HOLY WATER AND WHISKEY SCARS

ALI SPOONER

Affinity
RAINBOW
PUBLICATIONS

ALSO BY ALI SPOONER

SINGLE STORIES

I Am the Storm
The Ghost of East Texas
The Trophy Wives Club – TWC1
The Bee Charmer
Ruined
Back in the Saddle
Open Your Heart
South of Heaven
Shotgun Rider
The Settlement
Love's Playlist
Cowgirl Up
Twisted Lives
The Epitaph
Terminal Event
Bailey's Run

SERIES

The Island Series
Neptune's Ring
Venus Rising

The Hunter Series
The Devil's Tree
Bound

HOLY WATER AND WHISKEY SCARS

ALI SPOONER

Affinity
RAINBOW
PUBLICATIONS

2023

Holy Water and Whiskey Scars
© 2023 by Ali Spooner

Affinity E-Book Press NZ LTD.
Canterbury, New Zealand

Edition First 1st

ISBN:
ISBN: 978-1-99-104024-4(paperback)

Editor: A Koenig
Proof Editor: Lisa M
Cover Design: Irish Dragon Designs
Production Design: Affinity Publication Services

ACKNOWLEDGMENTS

I thank my fans for following my stories and providing great feedback and encouragement. Writing wouldn't be so much fun without you. Thanks to Affinity, Irish Dragon, for the cover art and the team of editors, readers, and publishers who continue to help me grow as a writer.

DEDICATION

I dedicate this story to my Mom, who lived through some of the struggles of this small community. You are and have always been my Guardian Angel.

TABLE OF CONTENTS

CHAPTER ONE

"Holy Shit." Faith Wilson cried loudly as her hand clutched the panic bar above the passenger's side door. Her left hand pressed into the edge of the dash as her butt cheeks grabbed for the seat. She cursed Logan's choice of leather seats as she felt her body sliding toward the driver's side. Faith looked at Logan. "You remember we have already made our delivery, right?"

Logan grinned at Faith. "Yeah, I know. I just can't help myself. I love fucking with these guys. They have tried to catch Lightning for years but never do. I don't plan to change that tonight." Logan pulled into the cover of thick trees and cut her engine.

Several long seconds later, they saw the blue lights flashing between the branches as the sirens echoed through the forest. Faith straightened in her seat and looked at Logan. Her dark eyes were shining with excitement. "Why were they even chasing us?"

"I was running about fifteen miles over the limit." Logan shrugged. "It really gets their goat that those buffoons can't catch me. I give them a chase every time I can."

Faith shook her head. "You know that's going to land you in jail one day. Or worse. What will happen when they buy one of the supercharged cruisers, Ms. Bronson?"

Logan laughed. "It's not the cars. Never has been. It's the skill of the driver and lack of confidence that has kept them from catching me. They've never gotten close enough to get a tag number or even a good description of Lightning." Logan reached down and turned a button. The crackle of a police scanner filled the truck cab.

"The Ghost has slipped through our fingers again." They heard an irritated male voice report over the radio.

"The Ghost?"

"That is their name for me. I disappear like a ghost when they get close. Those guys don't realize I know every inch of these state and county roads. Even some that are no longer on any map." Logan reached over to brush a strand of loose hair from Faith's face. "I can drive every switchback within three counties with my eyes closed and never hit my brakes. These guys need to slow down for fear of taking a tumble down the mountain."

"You are crazy. You know that?"

"I've been called much worse. It's what I'm good at. You didn't have to come."

"I need to meet the buyer occasionally, but you've made my heart race tonight with that chase."

Logan scooted closer to Faith. "I thought my incredible good looks made your heart race, or my sexy eyes?" Logan wiggled her eyebrows for emphasis.

"Oh, they do. But they don't compare to the sound of your tires sliding on the gravel as you take the curves at full speed or the rush of the guard rails as you brush past them."

"You have such a way with words, Ms. Wilson," Logan teased. She leaned into Faith and kissed her. "We can stay here and fog up the windows, or I can deliver you safely to your bed before the sun rises?"

"Is it safe to get back on the road?"

"Who said anything about getting back on the road?"

Logan smiled and reached down to turn the key. She eased the truck forward until they reached an old logging trail. She drove through the forest for a half hour before reaching a paved county road. Fifteen minutes later, Logan turned down the path that led past an abandoned church to a small house.

"May I cook you breakfast in the morning?" Faith asked.

Logan cocked an eyebrow as she looked at the clock and then at Faith.

Faith chuckled. "Do you expect me to sleep after that exciting adventure? Come on, let's go."

†

Faith locked the door behind them and led Logan into the bedroom she had grown up in. Orphaned at three, Faith had been raised by her fraternal grandparents. Her grandfather, a Baptist Preacher, held weekly services at the church across the yard until his death four years ago. Faith's grandma had died years earlier, just after Faith had graduated from college. Faith had remained in the city for a few years, teaching school until her grandfather fell ill, and she returned to care for him. The small township was filled with sharecropper families or others trying to eke out a living in the foothills of the Appalachians. A small general store and gas

3

station were the oldest surviving businesses in town, along with Miss Ruth's Café.

Logan's family owned the gas station and garage. Logan's father had given up on having a son after his wife gave him two daughters, so he taught Logan everything he had learned about being a mechanic. If it had wheels, they could fix it.

Faith spun Logan around to sit on the edge of her deep feather bed. She began unbuttoning Logan's shirt as Logan's eyes glowed with excitement. Faith pushed the shirt off her shoulders and lifted the sports bra over her head. The skin on Logan's broad, tanned shoulders was flawless, and Faith enjoyed the feel of her skin under her hands as she caressed her lover.

Logan's hands snaked under Faith's blouse and lifted it above her head. Her fingers traced down Faith's collarbone, through the valley of her cleavage to the front enclosure of her bra. Logan's tongue circled her lips as Faith's breasts were uncovered. She leaned forward to bury her face in Faith's skin. She parted her lips to take a breast into her mouth and moaned as her tongue circled an erect nipple.

Faith's hands were filled with Logan's short dark hair. She closed her eyes and enjoyed the attention Logan's mouth was giving her breast. When she opened her eyes, Logan was smiling at her.

"Mama always said I was a titty baby," Logan said as she caressed Faith's breast with her cheek.

"I am so glad you are. I love how you make me feel." Faith fumbled to unfasten her jeans until Logan's calm hands took over and slid her pants and panties down her legs.

"You are so beautiful," Logan whispered against her skin.

Faith stepped back and held out her hands. "You have too many clothes on."

Logan stood, pushed her jeans down her body, and kicked them away with her shoes. "Better?"

Faith nodded and allowed Logan to place her on the bed before lying on top of her.

Logan's hands and mouth were eager to hear Faith's moans of pleasure. Her hands cupped Faith's breasts as her tongue licked a fiery trail down to her center. Logan's fingers teased her nipples as Faith spread her legs, inviting her lover to feast.

Logan welcomed the invitation and took her leisure, bringing Faith to a climax with her face buried between her legs. An hour later, Faith curled up in Logan's arms. "I've missed this," she said as her fingertips trailed down Logan's jaw.

"I have, too," Logan admitted. "We've both been staying busy. Dad is slowing down, so I have to pick up the slack. You have a book deadline approaching, too, don't you?"

"Don't remind me," Faith said. "Let's catch a few hours of sleep, and I'll cook that breakfast I promised you."

"That sounds great." Logan set the alarm and kissed the top of Faith's head.

†

Three hours later, the alarm sounded. Logan rolled over to silence it and crept from the bed. She leaned down to kiss Faith. "I'm going to take a shower."

"I'll get breakfast started," Faith said as she sat up.

"I can grab something at the diner if you need more sleep."

Faith smiled at her. "A promise is a promise."

Logan nodded and disappeared into the bathroom. Faith climbed from the bed and stepped into her house shoes, smiling at the disarray of clothes across the room. Slipping into a robe, she collected the clothes and took them to the hamper. She took the roll of bills out of her pocket and stuffed two into her robe.

Faith was cooking breakfast when she felt Logan's arms circle her waist. "That smells good."

"You do, too," Faith said. She reached into her pocket and pulled out the bills, handing them to Logan. "I almost forgot to pay you for last night."

Logan accepted the money and smiled. "I'm almost embarrassed for taking your money. It's so much fun making the run. I should be paying you."

"You have gas and maintenance on Lightning to cover."

"This recession has hit folks hard, so we have to barter goods for payments. Don't buy any eggs or bacon on your next grocery run. Our refrigerator is getting full."

"I'll gladly take any fruit you get. It would be nice to mix things up a bit."

Logan kissed her neck. "You know that may upset some of your regular customers."

"Maybe so, but I think others may appreciate a change. I need to make some grocery runs for supplies. Do you think you can help me? I know it's your only day off from the garage."

"There is no one else I'd rather spend it with. What time?"

"Early if you can. I'd like to make the run to the city and make it back in time for deliveries," Faith replied.

"Is seven good for you?"

"It's perfect, thanks. Pour some coffee and juice, and I'll bring breakfast."

Logan plucked a strip of bacon and placed it in her mouth, and tucked the bills into her pocket.

†

Faith walked Logan to her truck and returned to the porch to watch her pull away. She sat in a rocker and sipped her coffee as the sun crested the trees. She sighed when Logan tossed her hand out the window in a wave. Faith had hoped that Logan would change her mind about moving in with her, but her resolve had remained firm. There was no doubt they loved one another, but Logan needed to stay close to her father. That thought pulled Faith's eyes to the church. The community couldn't locate a new preacher when her grandfather passed, so the church was closed. Faith had considered several uses for the building, but it remained uninhabited, with its doors and windows locked. Her grandfather wasn't a rich man by anyone's standards, but he left the house, church, and a few acres to Faith with a small insurance inheritance. With the money she had saved from her teaching, Faith was comfortable, and the royalties from her books paid the utilities for the house. During his last days on earth, her grandfather had spent hours talking to Faith. He shared with her how he had supported his family and the needy families in the community for the last ten years. The memory of her grandfather brought tears to her eyes and reminded her how lonesome it was living alone.

†

Logan took her time returning to their small town. The morning fog enveloped her in a thick blanket as she drove. She took a sip of the coffee Faith had sent her off with and felt a smile form on her lips. It was getting hard leaving Faith behind, but her commitment to her dad and the business called to her. One day she would accept Faith's offer to join her, but now was not that time.

She parked beside the garage bay and walked inside to greet her dad.

"Good morning, Dad," she called out as she refilled her mug from the fresh pot of coffee.

"Morning, Logan," he called from inside the mechanic's bay.

"What's on tap for this morning?" she asked. "Do you need coffee?"

"I could use a refill," Curtis replied, handing her an empty mug. "I'm working on rebuilding this engine for Charlie's tractor. Ray is bringing in his old Chevy for an oil change and tune-up."

"That Chevy is older than me." Logan chuckled as she filled his mug.

"We've kept it running for this long. There's no way Ray could afford to buy a new one."

"I can handle that if you want to stay on the rebuild. Does Ray still have a crib full of field corn?"

Curtis wiped the grease from his hands and picked up his mug. "Probably so. The damn corn prices are at rock bottom. What are you thinking?"

"I'll do the maintenance on his truck for a few bags of cracked corn if he can get it shelled. I'm sure Faith could use whatever he is willing to sell. Do you mind if I ask him about it when he comes in? I'll spring for the parts and oil if he agrees."

"He would be a fool to pass on that offer."

A bell rang in the garage to notify them a customer had arrived. "I'll get it." Logan placed her mug on the tool bench and walked back through the office to the gas pumps. A young woman was behind the wheel when Logan walked up.

"What can I get for you?"

"Fill it up, please." The woman handed Logan two twenty-dollar bills.

"Sure thing," Logan said and took the money from the woman. She was able to squeeze thirty- six dollars into the tank and walked inside for the change. The woman smiled as Logan handed her the ones.

"Keep it for a tip," the woman said with a wink. "Is there someplace to eat?"

Logan nodded. "Miss Ruth's Café. A quarter of a mile on the right. She'll fill you right up." Logan chuckled and walked away. She placed the bills back into the register and returned to the bay. "Some stranger for a gas up," she told her dad.

"I'm sure their money spends just as well."

"I'm taking Faith to town tomorrow for supplies. Is there anything we need?"

"We could use a couple cases of oil, some plugs, and filters," Curtis answered. "I'll give you the money when we close up tonight."

"I've got this, Dad," Logan answered. "I made a run for Faith last night."

Curtis frowned. "I know the money is good, but I worry about you getting caught."

"They haven't found anyone that can keep up with Lightning and me," Logan bragged.

"Don't get too cocky. That's usually what gets you caught."

Chapter Two

When Ray arrived, Logan discussed bartering her work on his truck for cracked corn, and he jumped at the offer. He was happy to empty his corncrib to prepare it for the coming harvest. "Let me know how many fifty-pound bags you can come up with, and I'll get you a good price."

"That's a lot of corn. I don't reckon I should ask what you plan to use it for."

"To feed some deer to fatten them up before the season starts," Logan said with a wink.

"As long as the money is good, I don't care what you use it for. How long will your service take?"

"An hour tops for an oil change and tune-up."

"I'm gonna walk down to Miss Ruth's for breakfast then. I've got a sheller in the barn. Can I drop your bags off tomorrow?"

"Tomorrow is perfect. I'll see you in a bit." Logan took his keys and drove the Chevy into the service bay. She popped the hood and smiled to herself. Logan was proud to arrange a deal for local corn for Faith. It helped the farmer and would reduce the questions of what Faith needed cracked corn for from the city folks. Faith took advantage of any opportunity to minimize suspicion of her activities. She had even considered buying a steer to fatten up for slaughter. Then she realized she couldn't stand to have a pet slaughtered for meat. She understood how critical raising animals and hunting was to her community, but she couldn't fathom the guilt she would feel. Logan's smile broadened thinking of Faith. She would eat a good steak or burger if there wasn't a cute face attached to it. She removed the plug to begin draining the oil and gathered her needed supplies.

†

Faith cleaned the kitchen and booted up her computer. She sipped coffee and stared at the blinking cursor. The words that generally flowed from her fingertips had grown silent. Faith picked up her coffee, walked back to the porch, and gazed at the wooden building with flakes of white paint beginning to peel. The fog had burned off with the rising sun, and her thoughts drifted back to her grandfather. She knew that her grandfather had provided groceries and needed staples for many of the families in his congregation but was clueless about how he could afford to offer them. The parishioners tithed what they could, which was very little, but he would make deliveries to needy families every few weeks. One night, just a few days before he passed away, he revealed a secret to Faith.

Her grandfather stood up from the kitchen table and offered her a hand. "There is something I need to show you." He led her into the pantry filled with canned goods given to him, and he moved a wooden box that was used to store onions or potatoes. Faith remembered seeing a small metal ring attached to the floor. She had seen it hundreds of times as she helped clean the pantry but had assumed it was some form of an anchor and had never questioned its presence.

"I need you to pull that up for me."

Faith had looked at him with a frown of confusion but pulled on the ring. She was surprised when a section of the floor revealed a door and steps leading into a carved-out room. He climbed down the steps and flipped a light switch that showed much more than a root cellar.

"What on earth?" Faith asked.

"It's a long story, but one you should know." He motioned around the room and the tunnel leading from it. "Originally, this house and the church were a part of the underground railroad. The home's inhabitants and the preacher sheltered individuals fleeing slavery while heading north to freedom." He started to walk through the tunnel. "This leads under the yard a short distance to the church and a similar room hidden there. When I discovered this, I began using it for a different purpose." He pushed a door open and flipped a light switch.

Faith gasped when the illuminated room revealed a moonshine still. She looked between the copper still and her grandfather's face with disbelief. "I'm afraid I don't understand."

"Come, sit with me, and I'll tell you the story." He walked over to two chairs, eased himself into one, and waited for Faith to sit next to him.

When Faith sat, she looked up at him. "I think I'm ready for this."

"You know we live in a poor economic community with very little help from the government. Most families here wouldn't have food on their tables if they didn't grow, hunt, or catch it. The farmers grew excellent produce, fruits, and berries, but the large farms made the market prices drop, and the cost of gas to deliver it to the cities wiped out potential profits, so it was easier to grow what you needed to eat and barter the rest for goods and services."

"But how does this explain a moonshine still?" Faith stammered.

"Logan's father, Curtis, has been a faithful deacon in my church for years. One night after a service, I told him about the church's secret and the underground tunnel and rooms. We had been lamenting the despair of our community for months, trying to determine a way to help our community."

Faith was beginning to piece the puzzle together but patiently waited for her grandfather to continue.

"Curtis' grandfather was a legendary moonshiner during Prohibition and developed highly prized recipes that sold well in the mountains and surrounding cities. After his passing, the family business died off, despite a steady request for the shine. Curtis' father was leery of going to jail and didn't feel the profits were worth the risk."

Faith could see a sparkle of excitement in his eyes that had been absent for months during his illness. She was about to ask a question when he resumed his story.

"Curtis and I devised a plan to rebuild his grandfather's still and business and call it Holy Water. We studied his journals and rebuilt the still here, and began experimenting. It wasn't an immediate success, but we learned the distilling basics within a few months. Once we began to sell the product, we used the profits to purchase the needed goods for the community."

13

"That's how you were able to help so many families in the community?" Faith asked.

He nodded. "Until I got sick. I would cook the mash, and Curtis made the runs to deliver the product." He smiled at Faith. "I know you and Logan have remained friends from childhood, and she has developed her father's extraordinary driving skills. My time is running short, but the needs of this community remain."

Faith's eyes grew wide. "Do you want me to become a moonshiner?"

"Curtis isn't getting any younger either, but he has the skills to teach you how to cook. He believes Logan would more than fill the need for a runner to make deliveries. We want you to continue the Holy Water legacy and support the community. Without it, our tiny community will wither and die." He sighed deeply. "I know it's a lot to ask of you, but this is my home as it is yours. The search for a new pastor has been fruitless, so when I'm gone, the church will be abandoned."

She could hear the despair in his voice as he spoke. Moonshine was still illegal, and they could face jail time if caught. "How have you escaped detection all these years?"

"We never became greedy. We'd cook twice a month, generating enough profit to purchase the items the community needed. We could have sold so much more, but it could have jeopardized our freedom. Curtis had a few close calls during deliveries, but the church has never come under suspicion."

"It sounds like a brilliant plan. Do you think I can learn to cook the mash?"

"I know you can if you're willing to take the risk. Curtis can teach you, and you will have my journals to use as a resource."

"Does the community know where the money comes from?"

"I'm sure they have their suspicions but would never question our generosity."

"You mentioned access from inside the church."

He smiled and nodded. "A similar bolt and door beneath my desk. I rarely used it, so it remained hidden by an area rug."

"Incredible," Faith stated. "I would never have thought all this was here in my wildest dreams." Her smile broadened. "Did Gran know?"

"Of course. Your gran was a tremendous help in purchasing supplies. She would go to town twice a month to buy our jars, yeast, sugar, and other items. If she were ever questioned, she would say that the ladies of the church were busy canning vegetables, making jelly or fresh bread. It was very believable, as she often organized these events for the church."

Faith saw him grimace. "It's time for more medication, isn't it?"

"Yes. I needed to talk to you about this. Curtis and Logan will have a similar conversation today and come out to discuss the plan after dinner." He stood and left the room.

Faith took a final look at the still and turned off the light before closing the door behind her. She followed her grandfather back to the pantry and concealed the door while he took his medicine.

"I need to lay down a bit, if you don't mind."

"Not at all. How about some grilled cheese sandwiches for supper? I know you like them, and they seem to sit well in your stomach."

"That would be perfect." He walked to a bookshelf in his office and pulled down a book. "Look through this if you want. It's our journal from day one. It shows lists of supplies, recipes, and other information that may be of help."

"Thanks," she answered and carried the book to the kitchen table. "Moonshine," she whispered and shook her head with a soft laugh.

†

Faith prepared some cookies and a pot of coffee for the meeting. She welcomed Logan and her father into the house. "Did you have a clue?" she whispered to Logan.

"Not even the faintest," Logan answered. "It's such a wild idea. I would never have guessed."

The four sat at the table, sipping coffee and munching on cookies. Curtis looked at Faith. "I would bet you were as shocked as Logan was today."

Faith nodded. "I never had a clue." She fidgeted with her napkin. "I wondered where the money came for all the goods given to the families but would have never guessed it was from Holy Water."

"That was your grandfather's idea. It fits the bill perfectly. I'm just thankful we never got stopped for inspection. That would definitely not pass for any holy water I've ever seen." Curtis chuckled.

Faith looked at Logan. "Can we do this?"

Logan shrugged. "I don't see why not. It's kind of a screwed-up version of Robin Hood. I'm game if you are. I can't imagine how our community would survive without the extra help."

Faith saw the worry in her grandfather's eyes. "When can we get started?"

"Saturday night, unless y'all have other plans," Curtis said.

"We do now," Logan answered.

"I'll pick up the supplies we need, and we'll start by showing you how to make the mash. We can cook and plan a delivery when the fermentation is complete."

†

Faith and Logan proved to be quick studies and quickly learned the process of distilling and packaging the product. After their first batch was cooked, Curtis loaded his truck and took Logan along for the first delivery. It was an uneventful run, but Logan was amazed at how much people would pay for Holy Water. "Was it ever tempting to cook more to make more money?"

"We were adamant about sticking to only what we needed to generate the revenue to supply the community. Faith's grandfather would see it as a sin if it were produced for pure profit." Curtis laughed. "He thought the Lord would forgive us if we used the money to help his flock survive. We only kept what we needed to keep us in supplies and gas for the deliveries."

†

That was how the "Holy Water" legacy continued after her grandfather's death. Faith and Logan had filled their fathers' shoes and continued to support the struggling community. The first time she and Logan made deliveries, relieved adults welcomed them into their homes. Many were surprised the deliveries continued, but they were thankful for the assistance. "We weren't sure how we would survive without your grandfather," many smiling faces told them.

"We will do our best to do what we can," Faith had assured them.

17

CHAPTER THREE

Faith's mind was too conflicted about completing any productive writing, so she finally gave up and walked into the church storage shed. She took out a small gas can and filled the weed eater tank. The small cemetery attached to the church could use some attention, and it would be weeks before the next scheduled maintenance by the crew of deacons that tended the property. The morning had remained cool, and the sun kissing her skin felt good as she moved from one plot to the next. Faith had finished trimming the second row when she looked up. An unfamiliar car had pulled up in front of the church, and a young woman was walking toward her. The woman was well dressed and smiled as she walked toward Faith.

"Good morning," Faith said. "Are you lost? May I help you with something?"

The woman shook her head and laughed. "Good morning. My name is Patrice Long, and I am with the school district. I'm looking for Faith Wilson. I don't believe I'm lost. Am I?"

Faith ran her wrist across her face to wipe away her sweat. Her arm was covered in dried grass, which stuck to her cheek. She swiped at it to no avail. "I am Faith Wilson."

Faith was surprised by the softness of the woman's touch against her skin as she wiped the grass from her cheek. "I would like to chat and share a proposal if you have the time."

"What type of proposal?" Faith asked cautiously.

"One that would provide a much-needed service to this community and a purpose for this building," Patrice said as she moved her hand toward the church. "I've heard this was your grandfather's church, but the doors have closed since his passing."

Faith squinted to keep the sun out of her eyes. "Yes, that much is true." She looked at the woman. "Would you care for a coffee or something to eat?"

"Coffee would be great, but I couldn't eat another bite after Miss Ruth's breakfast."

Faith nodded and started walking toward the church. She placed her weed trimmer on the steps and continued walking toward the house. "Have a seat while I get cleaned up. What do you take in your coffee?" She pointed to a cane-backed chair on the porch.

"A little sugar and some creamer if it's not too much trouble." Patrice graced Faith with a beautiful smile.

"No trouble at all. I'll be right back." Faith disappeared into the house and walked into the bathroom. One glance in the mirror made her break out a smile. The dead grass was gone, but a light coating of dust was turning into a mask of mud where it contacted the sweat on her face. "Well, aren't you a sight?" She

19

washed her hands and face before returning to the kitchen to pour two mugs of coffee.

Faith handed Patrice a mug and sat down next to her.

"Thank you." Patrice took a sip and looked at Faith. "I know this may be a surprise, but I have been tasked with finding an answer to a dilemma faced by this community for years."

"Which would be what exactly?" Faith asked.

"There are fourteen students in this community that are school age who ride a school bus over an hour one way to attend school. Unfortunately, many students from this area drop out of school when they turn sixteen. I won't mince words. It's hard for students in a struggling community to keep pace with their classmates. The teasing and outright bullying at that age can be brutal."

Faith nodded. "I remember. I was one of those students years ago, but I was privileged by being an only child living with my grandparents. I never had to go to school in tattered clothes and hand-me-downs. Still, it was hard being an outsider."

"You made it out of high school and went on to the University to become a teacher, correct?"

"Yes, I taught elementary school in the city for a few years until my grandfather's health began to fail."

Patrice nodded toward the church. "I would suspect the church has a few Sunday school rooms."

"You would assume correctly," Faith answered. "They haven't been used in quite some time."

"I would like to offer you a proposal," Patrice repeated. "I would like to team up with you to teach the students in this area using the church as our classroom. I am certified in high school education and could work with older students if you agree to teach the five elementary-aged children. The school district would provide all the needed supplies and prepare the rooms if you allow us to use the church. You would also be given a small salary and fringe benefits."

Patrice paused and took in a breath. "The prospects for these students are bleak, and with the economy on the downturn, I'm not holding out hope that the farms will remain profitable in the years to come. If we can prepare these children, there will be hope that they can improve on their lot in life by becoming better educated." Patrice took a sip of coffee. "I don't mean to offend you, but we need to do more for these children. I've done my research, and I know what this community means to you and what you mean to it."

"I don't disagree with you, but it's been years since I've taught. I've published a few novels and have savings and inheritance to keep me comfortable. The use of the building is not an issue. It needs some work done for sure."

"Which I could have completed over the summer before classes begin," Patrice offered.

"I'm sure there are better-qualified teachers than me," Faith said.

"I have done an exhaustive search to no avail. You know these families and their needs. No classroom teaches that knowledge."

Faith took a sip of coffee to let Patrice's words set in. Five students were nothing compared to the large classes she had previously dealt with. "This is a lot to consider. When do you need an answer?"

"The sooner, the better, so we can begin to plan. I could return Monday with profiles of the children and the curriculums you need to teach. In addition to the basics, I'd like to add some life-skills training for the older students." She watched Faith's face. "Teaching them math, simple budgeting, and employment

21

skills. The system hasn't done them any favors. A few will require remedial reading lessons to help them catch up."

Faith nodded. "Let me think about it over the weekend. You can bring out your profiles and plans on Monday for me to review."

Patrice nearly knocked the small table between them over as she jumped up from her chair. "I will start on it right away."

Faith frowned. "I haven't agreed to anything yet, except the use of the Sunday school rooms."

"That's a good start." Patrice stood and reached for her hand. "Thank you for giving this idea your consideration. I know we can do good things for this community together."

"Uh huh," Faith replied as she stood. She walked Patrice back to her car and picked up her weed eater. She returned the wave Patrice sent her as she drove away. Ironically, her grandparent's graves were the next to be tended. "Do I even need to ask myself what you two would recommend?" She placed her hand on the top of the granite marker. "I know you would remind me how important this little community was to you. Still, I'm not sure I want to get back into teaching. Is that selfish?"

When no answer came from the stone, Faith resumed her trimming. I will have Logan as a captive audience for a couple of hours tomorrow when we go to town. I'll run the idea by her to see what she thinks.

†

Logan added the final quart of oil to Ray's truck and checked the levels. He had arrived a few minutes early and was drinking coffee with Curtis when Logan walked in with his keys.

"She was quite the looker and was asking about the church," Ray told Curtis.

"Who was?" Logan asked and handed him the keys.

"Some city woman who stopped at Miss Ruth's for breakfast. I heard her asking about the church when I was paying my bill."

"That must have been the woman who stopped here earlier for gas," Logan told her dad.

"More than likely. I wonder what the woman wants with the church?"

"No telling. The woman looked high-class, so maybe she was a realtor or lawyer," Ray answered. "Will you be here tomorrow so I can drop the corn off?"

"I won't be here, but Dad will be around. Especially if he doesn't finish rebuilding that engine. You can wait until Monday if that's better for you. There's no rush." Logan wiped her hands on a shop towel.

"I'll be here," Curtis grumbled. "That dang engine is giving me fits."

"I'll help you, Dad," Logan promised.

Ray drained his coffee and dropped the cup in the trash. "I'll wait until Monday when I know you'll be around. Thanks, Logan."

"You are welcome, Ray. Have a good night."

Ray placed his hand on Curtis's shoulder. "Don't let that engine get the better of you."

Curtis looked up at him with a grin. "I'll try my best."

They watched as Ray drove away, and Logan turned to her dad. "Are you hungry?"

"I could eat," Curtis answered.

"You want me to go to Miss Ruth's for some lunch? I've got a hankering for one of her club sandwiches."

23

"I could do a burger and fries. Take some money from the till."

"Naw, Dad, I've got this. I'll be back shortly." Logan washed the oil from her hands and walked out to her truck. Lightning wasn't incredibly flashy to look at. She had a few areas covered in Bondo until Logan could get a proper paint job. She blended in well with the work trucks of the farmers in the area. What made her special was under the hood. Lightning had the top of the line everything, including a turbocharged chip that gave her even more speed. Logan had considered installing a nitrous system, but she felt that was only asking for trouble. As it was, she had been able to outrun any cruiser that was game for a chase. Logan had done the majority of the modifications herself, and Curtis didn't hesitate to tease his daughter about the money she had sunk into the truck. Logan climbed in behind the wheel and turned the key. The engine rumble made Logan smile, and she waved to her dad before driving off.

The drive to Miss Ruth's wouldn't even warm up Lightning's motor, but it was Logan's only option for a hot meal in town. She walked inside and sat at the counter until Miss Ruth came to take her order.

"What'll it be today, Logan?"

"One of your club sandwiches for me and a cheeseburger with fries for Dad, please."

"No problem. I'll get those started for you. You want a drink while you wait?"

"Just a glass of ice water, please," Logan answered.

Logan smiled when Miss Ruth returned with a tall glass of ice water. "Ray told Dad and me a strange woman was in here asking about the church this morning. Did you hear anything?"

"It seems like the woman was from the school district and wanted to talk with Faith about using the church for a school for the local kids. There's not but about a dozen left since families have started moving away, but you know they have a long ride every day."

"Too long, just to be harassed by the city kids for being country bumpkins," Logan said with a snarl. "I remember I couldn't wait to turn sixteen so I could quit."

"You dang near caused your ma to have a heart attack, but I reckon it's all worked out well with your dad. He brags that there's no one in the county that's a better mechanic than you. He swears if it has wheels, you can fix it."

Logan chuckled. "It's easy when you learn from the best. Sometimes I regret not finishing high school, but the feeling passes quickly."

"You seem to be doing okay for yourself."

"I don't want for much," Logan said. "The house has been paid off for years, and the station and shop keep us in some jingling money. We barter for things we need and provide a service for our community." She smiled at Miss Ruth. "Faith and I are making a town run tomorrow. Is there anything you need?"

"Not that I could think of, but thanks for asking." Miss Ruth placed their lunches in a plastic bag and rang up the order. She handed Logan back the change. "Thanks for your business. I hope you enjoy your lunch."

"We always do, Miss Ruth. I'll see you next week."

"Tell your dad hello for me."

Logan nodded and headed out the door. A look to the south revealed a bank of storm clouds forming. "I bet we get rain before this day is over." She raised Lightning's windows and stepped out of her truck. She heard an approaching vehicle and turned to see the sleek car from earlier as it passed by the station.

25

†

By the time Faith reached the last of the markers, her arms were aching from the effort. She turned toward the storage shed and saw the dark clouds rolling in.

"Dang, rain is going to make the grass grow quicker than I can cut it," Faith complained as she picked up the gas can and stored her tools. She sat on the front porch steps to enjoy the breeze that was bringing in the clouds. "At least we get a bit of breeze." Her gaze fell on the weathered old church. Faith understood how much this community and the people living here had meant to her grandfather. He risked his livelihood and freedom to generate income to help the area survive. Patrice was right. Several large rooms in the back of the church could easily convert to classrooms, and having a school there would further reduce any suspicion of the Holy Water production. They generally cooked on the weekend, so it wouldn't interfere with her teaching duties. *Listen to me. I already think that I will accept the position.*

The wind whispered through the trees, and when she heard the first raindrops hit the tin roof, she walked inside the house. If she was going to get a hot shower before the storm hit, she would need to get moving. If Faith was lucky, she'd get a hot shower and a decent meal before the weather threatened to take out the power. It didn't take much for the community to lose a power line to a limb, or God forbid, someone took out a pole to plunge her house into darkness. Faith had learned years ago to keep flashlights and candles staged throughout the house. It only took her stubbing her toes a few times in the dark to realize how critical they were.

Faith saw the steam forming in the tiny shower, and it reminded her of the fog that had enveloped Lightning when Logan left for work earlier that day. Just the thought of Logan brought a smile to her face. She was glad she would see her again in the morning when they drove to the city for supplies.

After showering, she walked into the kitchen and prepared a grilled cheese sandwich. It was her grandfather's favorite, and toward the end of his days, it was one of the few things his stomach would tolerate. "Here's to you, Grandpa," Faith said. Seconds later, the room plunged into darkness. Faith lit a small candle on the table and finished her sandwich and a cold beer. *I won't be tempted to stay up late watching television tonight, which was for the best since Logan promised she would arrive by seven.*

Faith stretched out on her bed and listened to the wind howling as it blew around the house. They were in prime tornado season. She was too far from the county storm siren to hear any warning, but as long as she had cell service, she would get an alert. Faith picked up her phone. "Almost one hundred percent. I should be fine." She set her alarm for six and pulled the covers under her chin.

†

Several miles away, Logan sat on a small loveseat. As a teen, she had taken the attic as her home, and she enjoyed the silence and privacy the space gave her. Logan still had to go downstairs to use the kitchen but the attic was otherwise self-sufficient. The large windows she had installed gave her a nice view of the dark cornfields when the lightning illuminated the night. So beautiful but terrifying at the same time. The powerful bolts of electricity raced across the sky like a giant spider web. One strike of anything living could kill, or a hit to a dry field or forest could set the area on fire. Logan listened to the howl of the wind and silently prayed there would be nothing more substantial. She remembered the startling sound when the tornado siren went off for the first time. The tower was half a mile away, but Logan swore the loud sound rattled her windows. Worried about Faith being so far away, she took comfort in knowing she had the cellar to escape into if needed. She and Curtis would huddle together in the small room underneath the stairs. Lord willing, the storm would pass through and wash everything clean. Logan set her clock and climbed into bed. Her thoughts led her to earlier in the morning when Faith slept curled in her arms after hours of lovemaking.

"Be safe, my love," she whispered into the dark.

†

Faith slapped at the alarm blaring on her nightstand. "Damn. I just got to sleep." She groaned as she silenced the irritating noise. It was still dark outside when she stepped into the bathroom and flipped on the light. "Thank goodness for power and a hot shower."

Faith dressed and walked to the kitchen to pour two travel mugs of coffee. She knew Logan would sleep until the last possible moment and wouldn't take time to make coffee. In the twenty-five years they had known each other, they had learned each other's habits, both good and bad.

She sipped the strong brew until Logan's headlights flashed off her walls. Faith tucked her purse under her arm and picked up the coffee mugs. Logan reached over and took the mug Faith handed her through the open window.

"Ah, my savior," Logan joked. "Thanks."

"Thank you for getting up so early this morning. That was one heck of a storm last night, wasn't it?"

Logan nodded. "I kept waiting on the siren to start blaring. Thank goodness it never did. That sound puts my teeth on edge whenever it goes off."

"I can imagine. Just the weather alert on my phone is jarring enough." Faith rubbed her bare arms. "Would you mind if I rolled the window up? It's kind of chilly out this morning."

"Do you want me to turn on some heat?"

Faith shook her head. "I'll be good if the cold wind isn't blowing in."

"Just let me know if you change your mind." Logan put the truck in reverse, and they started the drive to the city. "I need to pick up some supplies for the garage, too."

Faith took a sip and nodded. "That's fine. We have all day."

"Before I forget, I worked on Ray's old truck and bartered for several bags of cracked corn. He's got a crib full of dried corn that he will shell to prepare for the next harvest. I told him I could get a good price if he's willing to sell the lot."

"That's a fantastic idea. I love keeping any money we can in our community, and no questions will be asked."

Logan flipped on her turn signal. "That's the plan. He could set us up for nearly a year if he has as much as he claims."

Faith nodded, and they rode in silence for a few minutes. She was trying to think of how to start the conversation about the school idea when Logan turned and smiled at her.

"I heard you had a beautiful visitor from the city yesterday."

"Word travels fast in a small town." Faith chuckled.

Logan grinned. "You should know by now that Miss Ruth takes notice of any stranger and tries to ferret out who they are and why they are in our small town.

"So, what did Miss Ruth find out?"

Logan shook her head as she kept her eyes on the road. "Not much. Something about the woman wanting to use the church for a school."

"That's partially correct. Patrice, the woman from the school district, wants to use two of the Sunday-school rooms for classrooms. There is a growing concern regarding the dropout rates and the amount of travel the kids in our community have to do for school."

"That's a legitimate concern. I remember those long rides in the dark in the morning, and then it was dark before we made it home in the evening. A lot of bullying occurred, and I'm sure that hasn't changed. I couldn't wait to turn old enough to quit school."

"There are fourteen school-aged kids in our community. Five of them are elementary school age. She proposed that I teach them while she handles the older kids."

Logan slowed as she approached a stop sign. She looked at Faith and smiled. "Well, you are a trained and experienced teacher. Your grandfather would love to know the building was being used for such a good purpose."

"I have no problems with the church being used, but I'm not sure I want to teach again. Five kids are nowhere near the class size I'm used to, but I'm sure the kids will need a lot of extra attention."

Logan frowned. "I'm sure the kids haven't had the best opportunities to succeed. I hope you will give it serious consideration. I know you'd be great."

"Patrice wants to teach the kids the basics and some life-skills training. Cooking classes, budgeting, and other things high school won't prepare them for."

"I can help with that." Logan smiled. "I can teach them the basics of vehicle care. Checking fluids, air pressure, changing a flat tire, and the like."

"That's a great idea. Those sound like skills kids from this area need more than algebra," Faith said.

"I know a good general education is important. But there are also many other things kids from our small community need to learn. They will drive a tractor, work fields, or cook and serve at Miss Ruth's if they stay here. I won't mind having an apprentice if one of the kids shows interest in mechanics."

Faith smiled. "Thank you for being so supportive and having some great ideas. Deep down, I think this is the right thing to do. Just as important as helping families put food on the table."

"So, what's the next step?"

"Patrice is coming out Monday to bring out the students' profiles and, if I accept, begin planning. The school district will do the remodeling to turn two of the rooms into classrooms, and they will provide any supplies we need to get started in the fall."

"Another plus is you will have comfort knowing the kids have a good breakfast and lunch during the week. I doubt they get much before the long ride to school."

Faith chuckled. "They can even learn to make it themselves in the church kitchen."

"Just remember, you are in the driver's seat here, so aim high when making your demands. They need you more than you need them."

"I would love to get the classrooms wired for internet and get laptops or tablets for the kids to use. Much more internet-based learning is available today than a few years ago."

31

"That's the spirit. I recommend making a list of goods and equipment to turn this into a premier learning environment. I'd include one or two vans, so you can take the kids on field trips. You may even be able to hire a bus driver to transport the kids, adding a job to the community."

Faith looked at Logan in awe of her brilliant ideas. "Would you stay for dinner tonight and help me create some plans?"

"I'd love to," Logan answered.

†

It was almost six when they finally arrived home at Faith's after making their deliveries. Faith paid close attention to the homes that had children, and the appreciation they shared for the special treats tugged at her heart. If there was doubt about her decision, their love melted it away.

"If you want to pass on cooking, I'm fine with a sandwich," Logan said. "We've had a long day, and I know you must be tired."

"Spaghetti will be easy to fix. I can whip up a meal if you start making a list."

"Just point me to a notepad and pen. Hopefully, you can read my writing."

"I'm pretty sure I can decipher it," Faith said as she carried two bags of groceries inside.

Logan picked up the two remaining bags and followed her inside. While Faith put the groceries away, Logan retrieved the pen and notepad while Faith started dinner. She took a seat at the dinner table.

"Would you like some tea or a cold beer?"

"A cold one would be nice," Logan answered.

Faith pulled two beers from the refrigerator and twisted off the lids. She placed one on the table next to Logan and carried hers to the kitchen counter.

"IPads, laptops, internet, vans, driver, what else?"

"A food budget for two meals a day and a cooking class. Will you need any tools?"

"Naw, I can bring anything we need from the garage."

†

After dinner, they lay in bed, snuggling. "I appreciate all your help and ideas today."

"It was my pleasure, and I always enjoy spending time with you. Seeing your love for those families and the bright shine in those kids' eyes makes all the lost sleep worthwhile."

Faith turned on her side. "I know it's been a long day, but I have time for dessert if you're interested. I know you have to open the station by seven."

Logan turned to face her. "People still need gas on Sundays, and it gives me time to clean or catch up on little projects we are working on. I'd never pass on dessert, though." She leaned in and kissed Faith.

An hour later, Faith rolled over onto her back with a chuckle. "I do love your appetite for desserts."

"You are completely irresistible," Logan replied. "There's no way I would turn down any offer from you."

"How about I make some egg salad sandwiches to share lunch with you then?"

"That sounds great. I think you're due for an oil change and tire rotation, too. I can do those while you keep me company."

Faith turned her alarm on. "That would be great. How about I cook you some French toast in the morning?"

"Send me off with a sugar high?" Logan teased. "Sounds perfect."

Faith stretched out beside Logan, who wrapped her in her arms. "Sweet dreams," Logan said and kissed her softly.

CHAPTER FOUR

Faith cleaned up the kitchen and reviewed the list they had created the previous night. This all seemed a legitimate and fair trade for using the church. It would be hours before she would need to prepare the egg salad, so Faith walked into the pantry and disappeared into the tunnel. Logan had already delivered the corn they bought in town to the still room, so Faith decided to set up the mash for this week's batch. Faith smiled as she dumped the corn in a vat. *That's the last corn we will have to get from town for a while.* She busied herself mixing the ingredients until she checked the time. "Damn, where did the time go?" A glance around the area was all it took for Faith to realize all she had accomplished during her visit. "Time to shower and get cooking."

Faith shut the trap door behind her and retrieved a wicker picnic basket. She plucked a fresh jar of sweet pickles from the shelf and left the pantry. She placed the eggs on the stove to boil and assembled her basket while they cooked. A fresh loaf of bread and a bag of chips were placed in the basket. Faith spotted a package of cookies and decided to bake some fresh for Logan. Chocolate chip were Logan's favorite, so she would bake them while she prepared the egg salad.

The timer sounded, and she drained the hot water from the pot before adding fresh water to cool the eggs while she showered. Faith laid out a clean pair of jeans and a T-shirt to wear into town while the water heated in the shower.

When all her tasks were completed, Faith loaded her basket and drove to town. Miss Ruth's Café had a few cars in the lot, but the rest of the area looked deserted. Logan had placed gas in Ray's truck when she drove to the gas pumps. Faith saw the truck's bed filled with bags of dried corn and saw Logan and Ray talking.

Logan smiled at her when she stepped out of her car. "You can just leave your car there for a few minutes while I help Ray transfer these bags into the back of Lightning. He went straight home and began shelling when I promised Ray I could find a buyer for his corn."

"No problem," Faith said. She reached into her back seat to pull out the basket and carried it inside. There was one small, round table in the station, so Faith decided they would eat there. She sat the basket on the counter as she set up the table and grabbed cold drinks from the cooler.

Logan stepped inside. "Twenty-five bags should keep us in mash for some time."

"How much did you offer him?"

"Ten dollars a bag."

"That's a steal and a great bargain. Should I pay more?"

"No, it's gravy for him and allowed him to prepare for this year's harvest. If Ray has a need, I know you will fill it, but I think it's fair."

"I'll give you the money before I leave, and you can give it to him tomorrow," Faith said. "Are you hungry?"

"Starved," Logan answered. Her eyes lit up when she saw a plate of chocolate chip cookies. "You do love me," she said as she took a bite.

"Was that ever in question?" Faith teased. "I know how much you enjoy cookies."

"This looks great."

"I swiped two Sundrops from the cooler."

"I can provide the drinks for such a nice meal," Logan smiled.

"Eat up then. I wanted to get some gas, but I can get it later if I need to move my car."

"No need. We haven't been busy this morning. I've gotten a lot of cleaning and reorganizing done. We should be able to find a tool now when we need it."

†

Logan filled her car with gas and returned inside to ring up her charge.

"Don't forget to add the oil change and tire rotation," Faith reminded her.

"I'll add the supplies for the oil change, but the rest was labor. I reckon it's a fair trade for such a nice meal."

Faith laughed and handed her the money for the service and the purchase of corn. "What will it cost me for you to deliver the corn after dark tonight and place it in the still room? That's a lot of bags, and we never know when there might be some prying eyes."

"I'll place it inside the side door and then park to remove any suspicion. I can carry it into the still room and stack it after."

"Dinner and dessert then?" Faith smiled.

"Dinner for sure, but I need to spend some time with Dad. He's going to the farm to have supper with Suzy and her husband, but he always comes back a little off."

"What do you mean off?"

"Down, but not really depressed. I think it's because Suzy looks so much like our mom that it makes his heart ache."

"I can understand that. Maybe we should have your dad come to my place for a cookout or dinner. Nothing fancy, burgers or something."

"Thanks, I think he would enjoy that."

Faith picked up her picnic basket. "I'll see you later then."

"Yes, ma'am, you will."

†

Logan waved as Faith drove away and then turned back inside. She stepped inside the garage and looked over her dad's motor parts soaking in a vat. "I think it's time to start putting you back together." Logan began removing each piece from the cleaning solution and drying it with a shop towel. Curtis had already installed the new parts on the motor, so it only needed to be reassembled. She could feel a smile growing on her face. Putting things back in the correct spot could be difficult, but it was easy for her. The location of the part came to her when she picked it up and began to reassemble the motor.

The bell ding alerted her to a customer, so she walked back through the office. She stepped outside into the waning afternoon sun. "Hey, Miss Ruth. Are you heading home?"

"I am. I decided to close a bit early today. We hadn't seen a customer in an hour, so we closed the shop. Will you fill me up?"

"Sure will. Pop that hood for me, too. It's been a while since we checked your fluids." Logan placed the pump in the opening and started filling the car. She lifted the hood and smiled. The vehicle had to be pushing twenty years old, but the engine looked brand new. Miss Ruth only lived a few miles out of town, so her daily trips were probably the only miles she had ever put on the car. Logan doubted the vehicle had ever gone over fifty miles an hour. The oil was starting to turn dark, but she wouldn't need to change it for a while. She topped off the windshield wiper fluids and a touch of brake fluid. Logan heard the pump kick off and closed the hood. She ran the pump to an even ten dollars. "I think you're good on oil for a while. How many miles do you have on her now?"

Miss Ruth smiled. "She just rolled over fifty thousand last week."

Logan gave the car a once over. "We need to rotate those tires, so bring her back one day next week when we can keep her for a little while."

Miss Ruth nodded and handed her a ten-dollar bill. "I certainly will. You have a great rest of your day."

"You, too, Miss Ruth." Logan watched her drive away before placing the bill into the cash register. She planned to work on the motor for another hour, then close. It had been a slow day, but at least she was productive. Having lunch with Faith was definitely the highlight of her day.

†

Baking the cookies for Logan had gotten Faith into a baking mood, and she decided to bake a cake. They could eat off it tonight, and she would have something sweet along with coffee to offer Patrice the following day as they discussed plans. She whipped up the batter and put it in the oven as she planned the dinner she would cook for Logan. The aroma of the baking cake filled the kitchen and pantry as Faith sorted through jars for canned green beans and squash. They would do nicely with the rest of the meal she had planned.

Faith poured a glass of tea and decided to make a fresh pitcher. She turned on the radio for sound as she folded some laundry and waited for the cake to bake. When the sky started to darken, she began cooking. She knew it wouldn't be long before Logan's headlights flashed across her front porch. Faith knew Logan would turn down her offer of help, so she prepared dinner for Logan to eat a hearty meal before heading home.

She had removed the last pork chop and was working on gravy when she saw Logan arrive. Faith hurriedly set the table and poured glasses of sweet tea over ice. When the timer rang, she removed a cast iron pan of cornbread and spread a healthy portion of butter across the top. She heard Logan's truck pull into her front yard. She walked to the door. "Come inside to eat, and I'll help you when we're done."

"Are you sure? It won't take me long."

"It will go faster with two and help us make room for cake. Yellow cake with chocolate icing."

"I'll be right there." Logan parked the truck and jogged across to lock the door at the church. When she entered the house, she breathed deeply. "You've got it smelling good in here."

40

†

Faith lowered the last bag of corn to Logan, who made a stack. After Logan scrambled back up the steps, she closed the entryway and replaced the throw rug to conceal the doorway. "That should keep us cooking for a long time," Faith said.

"At least until this year's harvest is dried." Logan smiled. "I'm ready for some cake and a big glass of milk."

Faith reached for her hand. "Come on then. Let's satisfy that craving."

Faith cut Logan a large slice while she poured the milk. She smiled as she saw the excitement on Logan's face when she saw the cake.

Logan drained her milk glass and wiped the mustache from her upper lip. "That was tasty."

"I've got a huge section cut and wrapped to take home to share with your dad."

"He will love that," Logan replied. "I think I inherited his sweet tooth."

"At least you got his metabolism, too. You can devour twice as much as me and never gain an ounce. That's just not fair."

"Maybe once you start staying on your feet all day teaching, your metabolism will jump-start again. You've got to remember how physical my job is, and I'm on the move constantly."

"I know, and I appreciate all your help this weekend. I would be a mess trying to unload those bags alone."

"That's why you have such a good partner." Logan looked at Faith. "I hate to eat and run, but I need to get home to Dad. Will I see you this week?"

"Of course, you will. Maybe next weekend we could go into town to celebrate the new school. If you're interested?"

"That would be great. We haven't been out to an authentic restaurant in ages. My treat, though," Logan insisted.

"How about you drive, and I'll buy?" Faith negotiated.

Logan stood. "You have yourself a deal."

"I'm sure I'll see you before Friday night. Don't forget the cake," Faith said and offered her the gift.

"I would turn back around if I forgot this. That was really tasty. Thank you."

"My pleasure. I'll see you soon."

Faith walked Logan to her truck and kissed her goodbye. She returned inside for a cup of coffee and sat on the porch to enjoy the cooling night. The skies were clear, and the absence of light was perfect for viewing the stars. A falling star raced across the sky, and Faith made a wish.

†

Logan returned home to find her dad sitting on the porch sipping coffee. He smiled at her approach. "Faith sent you something sweet," she said and climbed the steps. "Are you good with your coffee?"

"I could use a refill," Curtis said and handed her his cup. "Will you join me?"

"For coffee, yes, but I couldn't eat another bite right now. I'll be right back," Logan said and disappeared into the house.

She returned with fresh coffee, a large slice of cake, and a fork for her dad. He smiled at her when he saw the cake.

"If she didn't have her heart set on you, I'd propose to that young woman," Curtis said, surprising Logan. He saw the look on her face. "I know you two have loved each other for ages, and that love has grown into a relationship. What I don't understand is why you aren't living together."

Logan eased into a chair beside him. She could feel the fire on her cheeks. She had no clue that her dad was so astute at picking up on her feelings for Faith. "To be honest, I'm afraid of screwing things up. What we have satisfies us, and I don't want that to change. We have been friends forever, and I don't want our friendship to be altered."

"Have you ever considered it may change for the better? You absolutely glow when you are around Faith. I hope I'm not an excuse for you."

"I'm uncomfortable leaving you alone," Logan admitted.

"You would only be a phone call away, and we'll still see each other daily at work."

Logan nodded. "How was your visit with Suzy?" She wanted to change the topic of conversation to something less uncomfortable.

Curtis swallowed. "She got your mom's good looks but not her skills as a cook. I will deny ever saying that if you tell her, but I appreciate her effort."

"My lips are sealed." Logan smiled at him. "I finished the motor assembly for you today. I thought we could put it back into the tractor tomorrow and see how she runs."

"Thanks. I appreciate that. Has Faith made a decision about using the church as a school?"

"Yes, she will accept the proposal tomorrow, if her demands can be met. We created quite a list together. I want to teach automobile maintenance basics to the older kids once a week if you can spare me a couple of hours."

"That's much-needed skills. Most kids today can barely pump gas."

43

"If one of them shows some promise, I thought we might take them on as a part-time apprentice if business stays good."

Curtis nodded. "That's not a bad idea. I'm not as spry as I used to be. It would be nice to have some young muscle around. I can run the station if y'all could handle the mechanics."

"I think that's a good goal to have. It would provide another job in the community, too." Logan took a sip of coffee. "Faith will ask for at least one van. Do you know anyone who might be good for a driver to transport the kids?"

Curtis thought for several long seconds, then his face lit up. "How about Miss Ruth's son, Toby? He buses tables and washes dishes for her at the café. Sadly, the government has turned its back on an injured soldier. He would be great and could still work with his mom."

"It wouldn't be many hours, but it would give him some extra money."

"That would be my suggestion once Faith gets a vehicle. You could teach the kids to maintain those vehicles as part of their training."

"That's brilliant, Dad. Thanks. I'll share your ideas with Faith." She shuffled her feet nervously. "We are going to the city for dinner Friday night to celebrate the school, but I'm sure I'll see her before then."

"When do y'all need to cook again?"

"Probably this weekend. I can make a run during the week to vary the delivery schedule. Ray brought in twenty-five bags of dried corn, so we could stay busy for a while. We will still need other supplies, but we won't need corn. It was a win-win for him and us. It clears out his crib in time for harvest and saves us from buying corn."

"I can work the store Sunday if you need to cook," Curtis offered.

"I don't think we'll be late, but I'll let you know for sure."

"Be sure to send my thanks to Faith for the cake. It was as delicious as ever." Curtis stood to walk inside.

Logan stood to follow him. "I will, and there is enough for two more slices tomorrow."

"I thought I might grill us some burgers," Curtis offered. "Why don't you invite Faith to join us?"

"I will, Dad," Logan said as she rinsed the dishes. "I'll see you in the morning. Rest well."

"You, too, honey," Curtis replied and watched her disappear upstairs.

†

Logan was driving the tractor from the shop when she saw Patrice's sports car pass the garage. It was still early morning, but she knew Faith would be awake and moving around. Patrice wasn't wasting any time in following up with Faith. Logan planned to wait until mid-morning to drive to Faith's to invite her to dinner. That should give them time to discuss plans for the school. "I can handle things here if you want to return the tractor," Logan told her dad.

"I'll be back in a bit then," Curtis said and climbed into the seat.

†

Faith heard a car approaching on the gravel drive and looked up to see Patrice arrive. She walked out to meet her. Faith shook her head when Patrice stepped out of her car with an

45

armload of files. "Leave those, and let's go look at the building." She dangled keys in front of Patrice.

Patrice smiled at Faith's suggestion. "Does that mean we have a deal?"

"Not yet. I still have some requests to discuss before I make a final decision." Faith watched Patrice's smile fade. "Don't worry, I think they are all necessary and doable. It will still save the school district a bunch of money."

"Let's see what we have to work with, and we can get down to negotiations. Lead the way."

Faith opened the door leading to the four Sunday school rooms. "There are four rooms to choose from. We can use two for classrooms, the others as a library and the recreation area. There is a full kitchen that I would like to incorporate into our teaching."

Patrice allowed Faith to give her a tour of the facilities. "I like your ideas so far. We have to go beyond normal classroom activities for these kids."

"I don't think it will take much to prepare the classrooms. Some fresh paint and getting the plumbing checked out. Will we be able to use these tables as desks?"

"I don't see why not. Most classrooms are moving beyond student desks. I think we will need two teacher desks for our use. We'll also need some computers and a copier."

"I have them on my list." Faith smiled.

"Let's look at your recommendations and requirements," Patrice said. "I can bring the maintenance superintendent out later this week to plan if we are good with that."

"Grab your files and come on in. If you're interested, I have a fresh pot of coffee and some cake left from dinner last night."

"I am definitely interested," Patrice said. "I'll get my files and be right in."

†

Faith could feel her heart racing as she entered the kitchen to place slices of cake onto plates and pour cups of coffee. She had dreamed of the school last night and was excited about the prospect. When Patrice entered, they took a seat at the kitchen table. Patrice placed a stack of files on the table. "These are the records of the five kids you will be teaching. I'll leave them with you to review if that's acceptable."

"That's fine," Faith said. She took a bite of cake and reached for her notepad. "We've already talked about some of the equipment, but I have much more to discuss with you."

Patrice removed a notepad from her bag. "I'm ready, but please understand I may not have the authority to approve some of your recommendations, but I will present them to the director."

"That's fair. Are you ready?"

"I think so. That looks like a healthy list," Patrice nodded toward Faith's notepad.

"I tried to think of everything needed to make this work. The most critical item is two fifteen passenger vans. We need to have a way to transport the kids on field trips and get them to and from school. We also need to hire a part-time driver, but I don't think that will be difficult."

"Would you rather have a small school bus?"

"No. For two reasons. First, we only have fourteen kids. Second, I know the jokes and stigmatism about the short bus being for *Special Kids*," Faith said and made air quotes. "We don't want our kids to feel like they are any less than any other student."

"That's an astute observation."

"I have another ulterior motive for the vehicles. I have a friend who is a mechanic, and I would like her to teach the older students some basic automobile maintenance, and she could use the vans for this."

"I'm not sure I can get a salary for that or money for tools."

Faith shook her head. "Not necessary. Logan will volunteer her time and provide any tools required. She hopes to gain an apprentice if one of the students shows ability and interest."

"That's smart on multiple levels. Could we also talk the café owner into allowing the students to get some on-the-job experience there? It would give her some free help."

"I think you will find this community will do everything possible to improve the chances for success for the kids. The General Store could also provide some training."

Patrice took a sip of coffee to hide her smile. "You have put a lot of thought into this in such a short time."

"I've just gotten started," Faith said and returned to her list. When she finished, she looked up at Patrice.

"I don't think we will have a problem getting your recommendations. The vehicles will be the hardest to sell, but you make your points well. I'll schedule a meeting with the superintendent for tomorrow morning. If he agrees to your requests, do we have an agreement?"

"Yes, I believe we do," Faith replied.

"I will call you as soon as I know. I'd like to bring the maintenance director out Wednesday so he can look at the physical plant."

"That's not a problem," Faith answered. She heard the sound of a vehicle approaching and smiled when she saw it was

Logan. "You are about to meet my mechanic friend. I'm sure she won't mind answering your questions."

Logan knocked on the door and stepped inside. "Sorry, I didn't realize you had company," Logan said.

"No problem. Logan Bronson, I'd like you to meet Patrice Long."

"I think we met, sort of," Logan replied. "You stopped in for gas last week, didn't you?"

"Yes, I did. Faith has told me about the possibility of you doing some teaching. That sounds like a fantastic idea."

"I'd love to teach general automotive skills using the vans if you can get them." Logan looked at Faith. "Dad recommended Toby as a part-time driver to transport the kids. It wouldn't interfere too much with his job at the café."

"That's a great idea," Faith agreed.

"I don't want to interrupt any further, but Dad asks if you will join us for burgers tonight?" Logan asked Faith.

"I'd love to. What can I bring?"

Logan smiled and nodded toward the counter. "Any of that cake you have leftover. He ate a large slice last night."

"That's easy. Around six?"

"That will be perfect." She looked at Patrice. "It was nice to meet you, and I hope we'll see more of you soon."

"I have a feeling you might. I think we are getting close to an agreement," Patrice replied. "A few hoops to jump through, but I think they are doable."

"Just let me know if you need help painting or anything," Logan told Faith.

"Thanks. You know I will. I'll see you tonight."

"Later," Logan said and slipped back through the door.

"She seems excited to help," Patrice noted.

"Logan was one of those students who dropped out at sixteen to work with her father. The kids were pretty brutal against us country bumpkins even back then. I didn't stick out as much as the others. My grandparents always made sure I had new clothes and shoes and would not hear anything of me dropping out of school."

"Thank goodness for that," Patrice said. "We wouldn't have this opportunity if you did."

"There aren't many kids left in this community, so I feel like we need to do everything to prepare them for success if they stay here or end up moving away," Faith answered.

"This community is blessed to have you."

"I have received my share of blessings from the people here," Faith replied.

Patrice stood and looked at the files. "I'll leave you to review those. I'll call tomorrow, and hopefully, we can put our plans in motion. The summer will fly by all too quickly."

"That it will," Faith agreed. She walked Patrice out to her car. "Drive safe, and I'll look forward to your call."

†

Faith poured a cup of coffee and returned to her kitchen table. She opened the first file and immediately recognized one of the names of the family she made deliveries to. Faith rarely knew the names of the children, but this seven-year-old Sadie Morgan, she did. She had an older brother that would be in Patrice's age group. His name eluded her. Sadie was always eager to take her hand when she brought the groceries into their home. Logan had always insisted on getting special items for the children, and Sadie enjoyed coloring, so a new coloring book and crayons found their way into the bag. Strawberry pop tarts also managed to be on sale. Faith could never remember seeing a father in the home, but according to the record, his name was Jerry, and his wife was Teresa. Sadie was in the first grade, and her attendance had been an issue during the last school year. Hopefully, the new school would help that improve. There was little documentation to explain the absenteeism or her performance in class other than satisfactory.

Faith sighed when she closed the record. It would take the first week to determine what the children's skills were if this record was any indication. She reviewed each of the five profiles. Three girls and two twin boys with an age range of six to eleven. The twins were Toby's sons, who were eight years old. Faith worried that she would need to teach the older students some basic skills to help them catch up to where their levels should be if the profiles were any indication.

Faith opened her laptop and started creating a profile based on what information she could skim from the school records. She recognized most of the names as families she had delivered goods to in the past. At least she would be someone the family may be familiar with. She would recommend to Patrice that they visit the homes during the summer months to explain the new school program and introduce themselves. She could use the information to add to her student profiles.

The afternoon burned away quickly, and Faith decided to bake a fresh cake to take to Curtis. If he was going to grill burgers, the least she could do was bake a new cake. There wasn't much left over from the one she had cooked the day before. She tucked the files away and prepared the cake mix for baking.

†

Patrice was attractive and seemed to be impressed with Faith. Logan wondered if her lack of education ever crossed Faith's mind. Patrice was well educated, dressed professionally, and had a secure career. Logan had no doubt Faith loved her, but she worried that Patrice would be too tempting for Faith to resist. Logan shook the thought from her head and walked back into the garage.

"What's next, Dad?" Logan needed to busy her mind and hands.

Ray dropped off some bush hog blades for sharpening. "Do you want to tackle those?"

"Sure thing," Logan answered and walked over to the grinder. "Faith will be out at six."

"Will you cook some fries to go with the burgers?"

"I'd love to," Logan replied and pulled on some safety glasses.

Logan worked on the blades for several hours until Curtis tapped her shoulder. "It's getting late. Let's call it a night and get showered before we start cooking."

"Go ahead. I've got about ten more minutes to be done. I'll lock up and be right behind ya."

Curtis nodded. "I'm going to drop a deposit at the bank. Just don't beat me home."

Logan grinned. "I won't. I promise to slow down if I see ya."

CHAPTER FIVE

Faith finished icing the cake and decided to shower. She felt her smile grow as she picked out a pair of jeans and a long-sleeved T-shirt. She felt confident that Curtis and Logan would have a fire lit in the firepit, but the temperature dropped several degrees after the sun went down. The thought of Logan warmed her, but she knew a cool breeze would cool things off quickly without a fire. Summer was well on the way but had not arrived.

She showered and dressed before taking the cake holder to her car and driving to Logan's. The sun had disappeared, and no other vehicles were on the road. She passed small homes with lights burning and several that were completely dark. Several families had abandoned the houses and fields they had worked for years. Others succumbed to old age and either passed on, or lived with family elsewhere in other parts, or in homes for the elderly. It made Faith's heart ache, but her small town was slowly dying. The sidewalks of the few businesses rolled up with the setting sun or sooner, giving the area the appearance of a ghost town. Faith shuddered at the prospect of real estate developers who would come in and buy large parcels of land for pennies on the dollar. Larger farms across the state were already strangling the life and profits of small farms, which appeared to disappear in droves each year. She would do everything possible to help her community, but Faith knew it was a losing battle against progress. The cities had no place to grow except outward, and she'd seen other communities disappear into subdivisions with five-acre plots of land.

Faith shook the depressing thoughts from her mind as she crested a hill and saw flames flickering in the fire pit at Logan's side yard. She pulled into the drive, lifted the cake carrier, and headed for the front porch. The door was open, and she could see Logan at the stove.

"Come on in," Logan called when she heard footsteps on the porch.

†

Logan turned to see Faith approaching, and her heart hammered in her chest. Faith would look beautiful in a paper sack, but blue jeans and a T-shirt made Logan melt. "You look fantastic."

"Thanks. You've got it smelling great in here. What can I do to help?"

"You can take the tea pitcher out to the picnic table. I've already got it set and condiments in place. You can take some cheese slices out to Dad, and I'll bring the fries as soon as this batch is done." Logan leaned away from the stove and kissed Faith as she placed the cake on the counter. "That looks like more than leftovers."

"I made a fresh one for us," Faith said. "Wasn't much of the other left." Faith picked up the cheese and tea pitcher. "Call me if you need help with anything." She watched Logan nod, then walked out the kitchen side door to the grilling area.

"I hear someone wants cheeseburgers," Faith said as she handed Curtis a small plate with cheese slices.

"We might as well go with the works," Curtis said. "Cheese for you?"

"Oh, heck yeah," Faith said. She began filling tea glasses. "Logan is finishing the fries and will bring them with a plate of bacon in just a minute."

"Great. These will be done as soon as the cheese melts. I wasn't hungry until I started cooking, but now I'm starving."

"The burgers look great," Faith replied.

Curtis opened the grill and began removing the warmed buns, placing them on a platter, then placing a cheeseburger on each one. Logan stepped out as soon as Curtis pulled the last burger off the grill. "That's perfect timing." Curtis smiled at his daughter.

"We make a good team," Logan stated as she placed the fries and bacon on the table. "Are we all set?"

"Dig in," Curtis said.

†

"That was a fantastic meal," Faith said as she dredged a fry through ketchup. "I haven't had a burger that good in ages."

Curtis smiled at her praise. "Hopefully, we can do a few more cookouts this summer. Logan tells me you're going to be busy setting up the school."

"Yes, I will hear tomorrow if the school district accepts my proposal. I would be terribly disappointed if they turned it down, but I'm confident it will be a win-win situation for all."

"Your grandfather would be very proud of you," Curtis told her.

Faith nodded. "I think he would be, too. The more I think about it, the more sense it makes."

"If we can do anything to help, just let Logan know."

"The maintenance director is supposed to come out Wednesday to discuss any needed renovations or upgrades. The school district will make sure they get done over the summer." Faith smiled at Logan. "It will definitely be a busy summer. I have to get back into teacher mode. Most of the kids are from families we deliver to, so I thought Patrice and I could visit them and explain the change of schools. It may go easier if they see a familiar face."

"I think the families would be delighted to have their children taught here instead of busing them into the city." Logan shifted in her seat. "I know I would."

"The student profile folders they provided held very little information of value. It's like these kids were invisible. Just a way of meeting their quotas." Faith could feel the frown growing on her face. "I don't know what angers me more, the lack of a fair education or the lack of potential prospects for continued life here."

Curtis poked at the fire in the pit. "I think the handwriting is on the wall for our little community. I don't know how much longer the few businesses and families can hold on without some hope for a better life." He looked up at Logan and Faith. "I know you two will land on your feet if that time comes. You've got good skills and great work ethics."

"People will always need gas and a mechanic's service. Even if we just sell gas to people passing through. If there is no community to support, we could always increase the production of Holy Water." Logan bumped shoulders with Faith. "You could try out those exotic recipes you've been dreaming about."

Faith closed her eyes briefly and took in the smell of the wood burning in the pit. When she opened her eyes, she looked at the clear skies and the stars blanketing the night. She saw the flashing red lights of a jet heading to one of the big cities. "We'll cross that bridge if it comes to it." She relaxed back in her seat, the smell of flowers floating on the breeze that had come up. Faith shivered and laughed. "I wouldn't call watermelon or strawberry exotic blends."

"Are you getting cold?" Logan asked.

"Just a chill. I enjoy the company, but are you two ready for dessert?"

Curtis smiled. "Now you're singing my tune."

Logan looked at her dad. "Do you want some coffee or a glass of milk?"

†

Logan walked Faith out to her car. Faith leaned back against the door as she reached for Logan. "Are we cooking Wednesday or Thursday night? The mash will be ready either night."

"I'm not sure I can wait until Thursday to see you again." Logan stepped forward and brushed a strand of hair from Faith's face.

"You never have to wait. You are welcome anytime." Faith pulled Logan closer. She could feel her trembling. "I hope you never forget that."

Logan nodded. "For a moment tonight, while I was waiting on you, my mind wandered someplace it shouldn't have."

Faith looked at her with confusion and worry written on her face. "Where was that?"

"I wondered if you would realize the difference between Patrice and me once you start working together. She's all educated and classy. I'm just a simple country grease monkey. She could give you so much more than I can even imagine providing."

Faith looked into Logan's eyes, and even in the dim light, she could see them shining with tears. "You've given me all I could ever ask for. You give me a love that I've never known before, and there is no one on this earth I would rather be with. Patrice and I will become friends, but nothing more. I've got everything I need standing right in front of me."

Logan let out a sigh of relief. "I kept telling myself not to worry, but I had to tell you what I felt."

"We've always shared our feelings with one another. The good and the bad. I think that has kept us friends for so long." Faith leaned into Logan and kissed her deeply. She never meant to give Logan anything that would jeopardize their relationship. They had been there for one another through thick and thin; nothing would change that. "Just promise me one thing?"

"If I can," Logan answered.

"Don't wait until we are ready for rocking chairs on the porch before you decide living together is right for us. I want to wake up next to you every morning."

Logan chuckled. "Have you and Dad been conspiring? He asked me why we weren't living together already."

"What was your answer?"

"It was two parts. Most importantly, I don't want to screw up what we have. Second, I don't want Dad to be here by himself."

"You would only be a call away, but I will wait for you as long as it takes. I'm one hundred percent convinced you are my one."

Logan pulled her into a hug, and Faith suspected she was crying by the way her breath came in gasps. She held her tightly, stroking Logan's back until she stepped back and wiped her eyes. Logan nodded. "I do love you."

"I know you do. We are meant to be together."

"We will be. I promise. I just have to come to grips with leaving Dad."

"When the time is right, you will." Faith smiled. "Will I see you Wednesday?"

"Yes, ma'am, you will. Text me that you've made it home, please."

"I will. Goodnight, Logan."

"Goodnight," she answered and opened the door. She closed the door and Logan watched her drive away as her taillights disappeared into the dark.

†

Faith watched Logan turn toward the house and then focused her eyes on the road. The weather was cool enough for deer to move about, and they never hesitated to run out in front of moving vehicles. A bright harvest moon shone through her windshield, and when she reached home, she sat on the porch and stared at it for a short time. A brisk breeze made her shiver, so she walked inside to an empty house, already missing Logan.

She turned on her laptop and wrote on her current manuscript until midnight. Writing felt good, and she promised herself she would write more tomorrow while waiting for Patrice's call. The words were flowing well, but her eyes were beginning to cross. It was time to call it a night and get some sleep. She would check on the mash in the morning and stir it, but Faith was positive the mixture would be ready to cook on Wednesday. She looked forward to the hours she would spend with Logan. They were in their own little world, hidden away from everyone while they cooked.

Faith climbed between the sheets and listened to the whispering of the wind as it blew around the house. She hugged a pillow to her chest, breathed in Logan's lingering scent, and drifted off to sleep.

†

Just before nine the following morning, Faith got the call she was waiting on.

"They took everything, hook, line, and sinker. The vans were a bit of a tough sell, but the superintendent agreed to our proposals and requests. Max, the maintenance engineer, will meet us at nine tomorrow, and after he finishes his assessment and gathers a team, they will start Monday."

"So, we are really doing this?"

"Yes, we are. Can we work on a few things tomorrow? I don't think it will take Max long. I want to start developing some breakfast and lunch menus to include shopping lists. I'd like to involve the students in every phase of meal preparation from purchase to the table."

"We can incorporate many skills to accomplish that. Reading, writing, math, and money handling. Learning how to budget, too." Faith was getting excited. "I'll be ready and have the coffee pot going in the morning."

"Sounds great. I'll see you then."

Faith's face was beaming as she opened her laptop and made a few notes. She searched the internet for enjoyable and educational locations in the city that could be great destinations for field trips. They could easily tie those into the shopping trips as well. She stayed so busy, her coffee had gone untouched and turned cold, and her stomach was grumbling with hunger.

She dumped her coffee and made a fresh cup. She removed some eggs from the fridge and made two fried egg sandwiches. She made a list of items she would discuss with Patrice the next day. Visiting the children and meeting families were at the top of the list. They would go together, so she could help break the ice in her community. People were wary of strangers, so having a familiar face and reputation might make their jobs easier. Faith was deep in thought when she heard an animal whimpering. She walked to her front door and eased it open. A small black and tan dog heard her and stared up at Faith.

"Where did you come from?"

The dog took a tentative step toward her with a noticeable limp.

"Are you hurt, little one? Let me get some water and see what I can find to feed you, and maybe you'll let me take a look." Faith walked back inside and filled a bowl with water. She looked for something to feed the hungry-looking dog and decided it needed the second egg sandwich more than she did. She walked through the door and sat down on the steps. She placed the bowl of water on the ground in front of her. The scared dog eyed her warily, but her thirst was compelling, and she took several steps forward. "That's a good dog." Faith spoke calmly, soothingly. She watched the dog drink nearly half of the water.

"Are you hungry?" She broke off a piece of the sandwich and held it toward the dog. The dog licked its lips, but it was apparent to Faith that the dog distrusted humans. "I don't blame

61

you. Who would abandon you like this?" There wasn't another house for miles in either direction, and it certainly wouldn't be the first animal dumped in the county. She leaned down and placed the bit of sandwich on the ground next to the water. The dog was close enough to Faith that she could see it was a very young female. "That's a good girl," she whispered when the dog ate the food. Faith broke the remainder of the sandwich into three sections and placed them on the ground. The dog returned to the bowl and gobbled down the rest of the offering. Faith sat back and watched the dog.

"What are we going to do now?" The dog sat and stared up at Faith. "I don't have any dog food or supplies, for that matter. Do you want to make this home?"

The dog's soft whiskey-colored eyes met Faith's. She whined and dropped to the ground, and crawled toward Faith. "I'll take that as a yes, but we'll need to get you checked out, and I'll need to buy some supplies. Will you trust me?" Faith reached a hand toward the pup.

The dog licked her fingers and then stood up in front of Faith. "Good girl," Faith said and reached for her head. The dog shied away at first, but when Faith's hand stroked softly down her face, she stepped forward. "What should we call you, besides dog or girl?"

Faith was surprised when a stiff breeze blew, and the church bell in the steeple rang for the first time in ages. "Is that you, Grandpa?" Faith remained silent for several seconds listening to the sweet sound of the bell. "You always said you were a Soul Finder of lost souls, and I do believe this young girl fits the bill. That's it. Your name will be Finder. Are you good with that?"

The dog let out a soft "woof."

"Okay, Finder. I'm going inside to grab my wallet and my keys. We need to get you to town."

Finder watched Faith stand and walk back into the house. When she returned, the dog hadn't moved. "Will you let me carry you until I get a leash and collar?" She bent down and picked up Finder. "Good girl. I promise you this will be a good ride."

Faith placed Finder in the passenger seat and trotted around to climb into her car. "Hold on. We've got a bit of a drive to make." Faith looked at her gas gauge and realized she needed gas to make it to the county line, where the only vet in the area had an office. "I guess you will get to meet Logan and Curtis," she said as she pulled onto the highway.

†

Logan smiled when she saw Faith pull up to the gas tank. Finder popped her head up to look out the window. "Who is this cutie?"

"I've named her Finder. Someone dumped her, and she found her way to my place."

Logan reached inside to pet Finder. "She's adorable."

Finder licked Logan's palm. "She likes you, too, apparently."

"Tell me you're not taking her to the pound?"

"Heaven's no. I've already named her, so she's family now. I'm taking her to see Dr. Carson to get her checked out and cleaned up while I get supplies."

"Hey, Dad. You need to come to see this cutie," Logan called out to Curtis.

"I see Faith all the time," Curtis said as he walked toward them. "Well, hello there. We've been blessed by two cuties today. Who is this?"

"This is Finder. She found me this morning, and I'm taking her for a check-up if Logan will fill my tank."

"Oh, shit, I'm sorry. I got distracted." Logan walked around to place the nozzle in Faith's tank.

"You know I'm just teasing you, sweetie. I don't want the office to close before I get there."

"Why don't you call while I'm fueling you up. That's a long trip if Doc Carson's not in the office."

"Good point." Faith pulled out her phone and dialed the number she looked up. She was thankful when Doc Carson answered on the third ring. She would be in all afternoon and would look forward to meeting Finder. "I'll grab a pizza to pop in the oven if you want to come out for dinner."

"You have a deal. And I have a pup to play with." Logan grinned.

"Stop it at twenty, please. That will give me almost a full tank." Faith dug out a twenty-dollar bill and handed it to Logan. "I'll see you later."

"Be careful and have fun with that pup," Curtis said.

"I will," Faith answered and pulled back onto the road.

She left Finder with the vet for a check-up, bath, and nail care while she shopped for food, bowls, a bed, collar and leash, and, of course, toys. Faith loaded the dog supplies and the pizza into the back of the car and drove home to pick up Finder.

†

Doc Carson led Faith into the exam room. Finder was wagging her tail so hard she almost fell off the table when she saw Faith. Faith stood beside Finder, patting her head.

"I think you've found your new best friend. Finder is relatively healthy, aside from being a bit dehydrated and malnourished from being abandoned. Nothing some regular food and water won't cure. She had a sandspur in between her toe pads, causing the limp. She's a clean girl now and ready to go home. I know you'll treat her well, and she'll be a great companion." Doc Carson patted Finder's head. "You be a good girl. I'll need to see her back in three to four months if you want to have her altered. Don't hesitate to bring her in sooner if you have any problems."

"Do you know how old she is or what breed?"

"She can't be more than three months old. I'd guess Shepard, maybe mixed with a Rottweiler, based on her color and markings. I don't think she will be a big dog, though."

Finder licked Faith's cheek. "You smell nice." Faith hugged her neck. "You ready to go home?" She placed the collar and leash on her and lowered Finder from the exam table to the floor. "How much do I owe you, Doc?"

Doc Carson smiled. "This one's on the house. Seeing that she will have a wonderful, loving home is enough."

Faith realized it would be fruitless to argue. "Thank you. I promise I will give her all the love I can."

"That's all anyone could ask for. Drive safe."

Faith nodded at Doc Carson and gently led Finder out to the car. She'd no sooner opened the door when Finder launched her small body into the seat. Faith chuckled, walked around the car, and climbed behind the wheel. She looked over at Finder and could swear the dog was smiling at her. "Let's go home and get you some food." Faith heard the thumping of Finder's tail against the door.

Faith drove straight home to feed Finder and get the pizza in the refrigerator. She didn't see Logan as she passed, so she assumed she was working inside the bay. Faith pulled up to the house, took the leash off the collar, and let Finder jump out. "Go potty while I unload the car, and we'll get some food in your belly." Finder trotted off, her nose to the ground in search of the right spot, then squatted to relieve her bladder. Faith put the pizza away, opened the bag of food to fill the bowl, and placed it on the floor for Finder, who had followed her inside. When she started eating, Faith unloaded the rest of her purchases. She put a bag of treats and toys on the kitchen table, carried the bed into her bedroom, and placed it beside her bed. Finder's head hadn't lifted from the bowl when Faith returned and filled the water bowl. "There will be plenty for later, so don't think you have to eat it all right now."

Finder ate a few more mouthfuls before stopping to take a drink. Then she sat beside the table, looking up at Faith as she removed the tags from the toys. Faith picked up a small brown teddy bear, hugged it tight to her chest to transfer her scent to the toy, and then offered it to Finder. Finder took it gently from her hand and lay down, placing her head on the stuffed bear.

"That's a good girl," Faith told her. She placed the toys across the table. "I think I went a bit overboard," Faith said with a chuckle. Faith walked to the fridge for a glass of tea, and Finder's eyes followed her every move. "Let's go outside for a bit." She picked up a chew stick and a ball.

Finder stood and looked between Faith and her bear. "You can bring bear." Finder took it in her mouth and followed Faith outside. She sat on the porch steps and took a sip of tea as Finder settled beside her. Faith offered her a chew stick and smiled as Finder started to gnaw on the crunchy treat.

Faith took another drink and looked across the yard at the church. The bell hung motionless in the steeple. "Thank you, Grandpa. I think she's a good addition." Faith expected the bell to ring but was surprised by a gentle breeze that blew across her skin. It was as soft as her grandfather's caress when he talked to her, and she knew he was with her in spirit. Faith reached over to stroke Finder's body. She closed her eyes and enjoyed the cool breeze and the softness of Finder's coat between her fingers. Her eyes flew open when she felt Finder's body tense.

Finder had spotted a squirrel as it hopped across the yard looking for acorns or pecans buried in the grass. Her ears perked up, and Faith could feel the quivering of the pup's body as she watched the squirrel. "Go ahead. You know you want to chase him."

Finder launched off the steps and rushed after the squirrel. The squirrel easily evaded the chase to climb the tree and bark at the dog, scolding her for the pursuit. Finder turned to look at Faith. "You'll have to be much faster to catch a squirrel." At the sound of her voice, Finder trotted back toward her and lay at her feet. Faith offered her the chew stick, and Finder returned to crunching on the tasty treat.

When the sun began to sink, Faith returned inside. She found a small wicker basket in the closet to place Finder's toys. She sat the basket on the floor next to her recliner and returned to the kitchen. Logan would be on her way soon, so Faith turned the oven to pre-heat and checked her pitcher of iced tea.

†

Logan locked the door and gave her dad a hug. "I'll be late tonight, but I'll try to be quiet."

"Don't worry about that. I won't rest easy until I hear your feet on the stairs. Be careful, and don't take any unnecessary risks."

Logan nodded as they walked toward their trucks. "Have a good night. I'll see you in the morning." She climbed inside Lightning and listened to the purr of the motor before putting the truck in gear. The air was cooling as she drove to Faith's, and she could smell the sweetness of the honeysuckle on the air. There was a new moon, so the night would remain dark, making it perfect for a run. "Perfect," she spoke aloud as she neared Faith's driveway.

✝

Faith had left the front door open to allow the breeze to blow through the screen door. Finder lifted her head when she heard the crunch of the tires and stalked to the door, her hackles raised. Faith watched her as Logan approached, and Finder recognized her and wiggled her rear end with excitement.

When Logan saw her at the door, she called out to the pup. "Hey, Finder, are you protecting Mama?"

"She heard you arrive before I did," Faith called from the kitchen. "She rushed to the door to see who was coming on her property."

"That's a good girl," Logan said and knelt down to pet the dog. She was rewarded by a soft tongue licking her cheek.

"Don't get all my sugar," Faith teased. "I was about to put the pizza in the oven. Do you want to load up while we're waiting?"

"We can do that. I'll hand the cases and buckets up to you, and then we can load the truck," Logan said as she walked into the pantry and descended the stairs.

Faith placed the pizza in the oven and set the timer. Logan handed her three cases of filled jars and then two five-gallon buckets. Logan carried the two buckets to Lightning. She placed

68

the buckets beside the truck then she opened the back door. The rear seat was replaced by a surface that held two massive speakers. Logan did like her music loud, but the speakers concealed hidden storage space. Logan pushed a button beneath the passenger seat to release a door to reveal the opening. She placed the two buckets deep into the area and then the three cases of jars. Logan surrounded the cases with a heavy blanket to muffle any noise and protect the boxes from shifting. She sealed the door and turned to Faith. "All set."

†

"Thanks for a great dinner. I'll see you sometime tomorrow to drop off the payment."

"Please be safe," Faith implored. "Do you want me to come to town tomorrow?"

"Naw, I'll drop the money to you after work if that's okay."

"Will you stay the night?"

Logan smiled. "That could be arranged." She smiled at Finder. "You have a good night and guard Mama."

Finder's tail thumped against the back of the couch.

"Come on, let's take you outside to potty before bed." Faith reached for the leash, and Finder rushed over to her. They walked out with Logan, and after another kiss, Logan climbed into Lightning and drove away. Faith waited until she disappeared to remove Finder's leash. "Go find your spot," Faith told Finder as she sat on the steps. She stared out at the moonless night perfect for Logan's run. She and Lightning would cut through the dark night like the Ghost, they called her. Finder trotted around the front yard and came to sit beside Faith.

69

"Welcome home, baby girl. I hope you will sleep well tonight. I know I will," Faith told her as her hand stroked down Finder's head.

†

Logan drove an hour to the assigned drop box for the week. She turned off the road and located the lockbox removing the payment envelope. Logan counted it quickly, then drove another mile down the road to a small trail. She turned onto it, unloaded the Holy Water, and snapped the padlock on the lid. The song of the crickets filled the night as she walked back to the truck. Lightning eased back on the trail until Logan reached the highway. Another successful delivery was made. Logan lowered the windows and let the chilled air flow through the truck. She hadn't seen another vehicle on the road since she'd left Faith's and was surprised to see headlights ahead. Logan eased off the gas and sighed when a passenger car drove past her. She picked up speed and went home without incident. The porch light was on when Logan pulled into the yard. She eased through the front door and locked it before turning out the light. There was enough light for Logan to see the path to the stairs.

"Welcome home," Curtis called from his bedroom.

"Goodnight, Dad. Get some sleep, and I'll see you in the morning."

"You, too, honey. I'll have coffee and breakfast ready when you come down. I love you."

"Love you, too," Logan answered and climbed the stairs. She stripped off her clothes and took a quick shower to wash the day from her skin. When she finally climbed into bed, Logan welcomed the sensation of soft sheets against her bare skin.

70

†

Faith locked the front door and picked up Finder's bear before entering the bedroom. Finder followed her, and when Faith dropped the bear into the dog bed, Finder curled up and placed her head on the soft toy. "Good girl," Faith said. She changed into a sleep shirt and stretched out on the bed. A dim night-light lit the room enough for Faith to see the dog bed. Finder was resting quietly and seemed content.

"Be safe," Faith whispered into the dark room. She looked at the clock. Logan should have made the drop and would be on her way home.

CHAPTER SIX

Finder flew out the door as quickly as Faith opened it the following day. "Good girl," she praised as she pulled the robe around her body and watched the young dog relieve her bladder. Finder trotted around the yard, her nose to the ground to track down the scent of any visitors. When she was confident her home was safe, she returned to Faith. "Is everything well?" Finder licked the hand Faith offered her. Faith smiled at Finder's soft tongue against her palm. "You did so well. Are you ready for some breakfast?" Finder followed her back into the house. Faith refreshed her water bowl, placed kibble in the other, and then turned on the coffee pot before returning to her room.

A long, hot shower was exactly what Faith needed, and after she dressed, she walked into the kitchen for coffee. Her eyes landed on the last sliver of cake she had devoured for her breakfast. Patrice and the engineer would be arriving soon to inspect the classrooms and facilities. Faith couldn't remember the man's name, so she hoped Patrice would come beforehand to refresh her memory. She poured a fresh cup and picked up a small ball, and with Finder on her heels, she walked back onto the porch and sat on the steps. Faith showed the ball to Finder. "Let's see if you know how to fetch. Are you ready?"

Finder stared at Faith as her body wiggled with excitement. She watched as Faith threw the ball and then turned to race after it, clumsily knocking it farther away with her paws. "Keep going. You'll get it," Faith called out. Finder pounced on the ball and trapped it between her front feet. She picked it up and carried it back to Faith. "That's a very good girl," Faith praised her. Finder placed the ball in Faith's hand and let out a soft woof. "Are you ready to go again?" Faith tossed the ball a bit farther this time, and Finder chased it down quickly and retrieved it. She trotted back to Faith and placed it in her hand. "You are such a smart girl," Faith praised. She shook her head when Finder's mouth formed a smile. "Again?"

They played fetch for about ten minutes before Finder got winded. "Time for a break," Faith told her, and Finder stretched out on the steps. "I'll be right back," Faith said and returned inside. She refilled her coffee and poured a bowl of water for Finder. "Take a drink," she told her as she sat the bowl on the bottom step. Finder lapped at the cool water, climbed beside Faith, and placed her head in Faith's lap. "You are such a good girl," Faith said as she petted the dog. She was nearly finished with her coffee when Finder alerted her to a car coming down the drive. Faith looked up to see Patrice driving toward them.

Patrice parked beside Faith's car and walked toward them. "I didn't realize you had a dog."

"I didn't until yesterday when she showed up. Patrice, this is Finder."

73

Finder's tail thumped against the wooden porch floor when she heard her name.

Patrice sat on a lower step. "She's a cutie."

"Smart as a whip, too. Finder's already learned how to fetch."

Patrice stroked down the pup's side. "Is that so? She's cute and smart," Patrice cooed to the dog. "I bet she'll be a good companion for you."

"There's no sneaking up on me when she's around. She heard you coming down the drive before I did."

"That's not a bad thing. Especially since you're all alone out here. I'm not sure I could live so isolated."

"I enjoy the peace and quiet."

"Enjoy it while you can. It won't be quiet with the furry kid around," Patrice teased.

"Will there be a problem with Finder being in the classroom if she chooses?"

"No, not at all. I think Finder would be good for the students. It could teach them some responsibility, and she will have someone with equal energy to play with."

"That's an excellent point. Doc Carson doesn't think she'll be big. I've always heard the runt of the litter is the best dog."

"I've heard that, too."

Finder's ears perked up again, and seconds later, Faith saw a truck coming down the drive.

"That must be Max," Patrice said.

"Max. I've been trying to remember the name all morning." Faith chuckled.

A handsome young man stepped out of the truck and walked toward them with a clipboard. "Good morning, ladies. I'm

Max Coffield from the school district. I've come to evaluate your building for classroom renovations."

"I'm Patrice Long, and this is Faith Wilson. We will be teaching together in the fall."

"Who is this pretty little lady?" Max asked.

"This is Finder. She made this place her new home yesterday," Faith answered. "May I offer y'all some coffee?"

Max shook his head. "Maybe after the inspection, if that's okay?"

"Fine with me. Let me grab my keys."

†

Three hours later, Max left with a detailed plan for painting the classrooms and updating some of the plumbing and electrical systems. If his plans were approved, the crew would start in two weeks, and the project would take another two to three weeks to complete, barring any complications.

Faith looked at Patrice. "We will be well into the summer before our classrooms are ready."

"If you allow us to use your kitchen table, we can complete quite a few tasks."

"That's no problem. I'd like to go ahead and make some lesson plans, at least for the first session," Faith answered. "I think we need to take this time to start meeting the students and families to let them know of the changes for the upcoming school year."

"That's a good idea. Should we divide and conquer?"

Faith shook her head. "I believe we should go together. They will recognize my face and maybe will be a bit more at ease. This is a close-knit community, and they are wary of strangers."

"Okay. I get that. Do you want to pencil in a schedule for next week? I know two homes have multiple students, so that will make it easier. Then I'll leave you to arrange the meetings. Should we go to them or plan to meet here before renovations start?"

"I think our initial visits should be in their homes to make them more comfortable. Maybe we can have an open house once our classrooms are set up before the school year begins."

"That's a great idea. We have nine families to visit then?"

"Maybe two per day and then three on Friday to knock them all out next week? I think that's doable. During our visits, I'd also like to see if there is any interest in the mothers to assist with field trips. I don't believe any of them have ever been given the opportunity, and I think it would go a long way toward investing their energy for their children to succeed."

"That's a good point and an excellent suggestion. Maybe we can plan some special holiday events, too, with their help." Patrice smiled, and her eyes lit with excitement.

"I've thought that maybe some of the older students can do some shopping for our meal supplies, and learn some valuable skills from menu planning to budget and money handling. Maybe we can schedule it with a fun activity in the city while we're there." Faith looked at Patrice. "There is much more than basic educational skills we need to prepare them for."

Faith realized that most students' potential to go beyond high school was extremely limited. They would be successful if they all graduated, and maybe one or two went to college. Perhaps she should consider starting a college fund using some of the profits from the Holy Water sales. If they determined an interest, she and Patrice could also begin teaching the students who wanted to go further how to apply for grants, student aid, and scholarships. With their economic situation, it would be worth a shot. Who knew, perhaps a student would want to become a teacher and eventually take over duties from her or Patrice.

Patrice was looking at her. "Where did you go just now?"

"I was daydreaming that maybe one of the students would go further and become a teacher."

"That's a possibility. One of the older girls has been a straight 'A' student for many years and is exceptionally bright according to her tests."

Faith frowned. "Are we doing the right thing by pulling her from her current school? We don't have athletics or after-school clubs to offer."

"They wouldn't be able to participate unless they could provide their own transportation, but you make a good point. The three high school students need to be offered a choice."

"If they were to choose to continue to go to the city school, would that interfere with our plans here?"

"I will get some clarity, but I don't think so. It would just lower our class size," Patrice answered.

They both resumed making notes until the silence between them was broken by the growling of Faith's stomach. Patrice broke out laughing. "I think it's time for us to take a break. May I treat you to a late lunch at Miss Ruth's?"

"That sounds lovely," Faith answered. "I need to take Finder out first."

"Take your time. I'll keep making notes."

"Come on, girl," Faith called to Finder.

Finder trotted to the door to meet Faith, and they walked outside. Faith realized this would be a test for Finder. "I have to go to town for a bit. Are you okay outside, or would you rather stay inside?" Faith knew they wouldn't be gone long, so she was happy when Finder followed her back inside. "Guard the house," Faith told her, giving her a chew stick to gnaw while they were gone.

"I'll drive," Patrice said as they left the house.

Faith turned for a final look at Finder to see she was stretched out, enjoying the chew stick. She turned to find Patrice smiling.

"Is this the first time she's been home alone?"

"Yes." Faith nodded.

"I can pick something up and bring it back if that's easier."

Faith shook her head. "I have to leave her alone sometime. No time like the present."

They climbed into Patrice's car and drove to town.

†

Miss Ruth looked up when they walked inside. "Pick a booth, and I'll bring you menus."

"Thanks, Miss Ruth," Faith answered and ushered Patrice to a booth.

"What can I get you ladies to drink?"

"Sweet tea, please," Patrice answered.

"Double that," Faith said.

Miss Ruth brought menus and two glasses of tea. "I hear you two are starting a school at the church."

Faith smiled at Patrice. "Word travels fast in a small town. Yes, Miss Ruth, we are. After we place our orders, could you join us for a few minutes?"

"I reckon so since no one else is going to come in."

"We have something to ask you." Faith smiled. "I'll have a club and fries."

"That does sound good."

Miss Ruth hollered back to the kitchen. "Two clubs with fries."

Faith scooted over in the seat to allow Miss Ruth to join them.

"So, what's up. I hope you don't need money. I'm barely scraping by," Miss Ruth stated.

"Two things, actually. Do you think you could spare Toby for a few hours a day to pick up the school kids and return them home after school? It won't pay much, but it'll be some jingle in his pocket."

"Yeah, I don't see a problem with that. What's the second question?"

"We plan to teach the older kids some job skills, and we'd like to know if one or two students can volunteer to work here a day or two a week to get some experience? No costs to you."

"They could work for tips," Miss Ruth said. "I'll provide them a meal, too. We aren't that busy after lunch, so could they come in first thing when we're actually busy?"

"I believe that could be arranged," Patrice answered.

"I think what y'all are doing is great for these kids. They don't have much of a future at the city schools."

"Order up," the cook called out and placed two plates in the serving window.

Miss Ruth retrieved their food. "Just keep me posted when school starts."

"One last thing," Patrice said. "Could you have them fill out an application and be interviewed to make it realistic?"

"Now, we're stretching it a bit. I don't have an application. Can you create a basic one?"

"We certainly can, Miss Ruth," Faith promised. "We can even write interview questions for you if that will help."

"I may need to attend this school." Miss Ruth winked at Faith. "Enjoy, and give me a holler if you need anything."

79

"Just more sweet tea in a bit. Is Toby around? I'd like to ask him about driving if it's okay with you."

"He's washing dishes. I'll send him out when you're done eating, so you can eat in peace." Miss Ruth chuckled and walked back to the kitchen.

Patrice wiped her face. "I don't think I've ever tasted a club sandwich this good."

"'Cause it's made with love." Faith grinned.

As promised, Miss Ruth sent Toby out when they were almost done. Faith watched the lanky man limp across the room. She could tell he was tired by how prominent his limp was.

"Hey, Toby. This is Patrice, and she and I will be opening a school at the church this fall. We're looking for a van driver to pick up all the kids and take them home after school. Are you interested?"

"Heck yeah, when can I start?"

"Not for a couple of months yet, but we wanted to see if you're interested. It will only be minimum wage, but it will be an easy job for you. Miss Ruth said she could spare you for a couple hours a day."

"That's perfect. Just let me know when you need me to start. My license is good, and I like kids, so this will be fun."

"All right then, that's settled. Will you ask your mom for a check? We'll be on our way, but we'll keep you posted. We probably need to make a run or two before school starts."

"Just say when and I'll be there. Thank you, Faith. Nice to meet you, Patrice."

"Same here, Toby. I look forward to working with you."

Toby returned to washing dishes, and Miss Ruth brought out the check. "You certainly made Toby's day. Mine, too."

Patrice handed Miss Ruth a twenty. "You made my day with that meal. It was delicious."

"I'm happy you enjoyed it. Hang on, and I'll be back with your change."

Patrice shook her head. "No need. Thank you, Miss Ruth."

When they got back to the car, Patrice asked. "I noticed Toby has a limp. Will he be okay to drive?"

Faith nodded. "He lost his left leg in the military. He's got a prosthetic device, but being on his feet all day at the diner can take a toll on him. He drives fine and can physically do anything we need him to do. He's got a heart of gold."

"Just like his mom."

"Yes, just like his mom." Faith sat beside her. "Thanks for lunch."

"My pleasure."

†

Faith found Finder waiting for her when they returned home at the front door. She raced outside to relieve herself and then rushed back into the house for her ball. Faith looked around to find the place in good order and followed her to the porch. "Good girl," she told Finder and took the ball in her hand. "You better get comfortable. This could take a few minutes." Faith hurled the ball and sat on the steps as Finder chased down the ball.

"She's a smart cookie. Finder has learned that in less than two days."

Faith nodded. "It only takes showing her once, and she catches on."

"I bet she could learn all kinds of tricks," Patrice said. "The kids are going to love having her in the classrooms."

81

"Finder will love all the attention, too, I'm sure. She loves meeting new people." Faith tossed the ball for ten minutes until Finder got winded. "Okay, little one. You need a drink and a break to catch your breath. Logan will come by later, and I'm sure she'll want to play." She accepted a kiss from Finder and started laughing.

"Logan is attractive," Patrice said.

"We've been best friends for a very long time. You won't find a better person than her. People around here love her."

"Including you?" Patrice asked with a grin.

"Including me. I hope one day she'll join me here full-time."

"Have you asked?"

"Of course I have. Logan's not ready to leave her dad alone."

"I just hope she doesn't make you wait too long. Are you up for another hour of planning?"

Faith nodded. "I am. We've made a lot of progress today. I'll start making calls tomorrow to set up our meetings."

Patrice nodded as she sat at the table. "That sounds good. I'll start on some menus and supply lists while you do that. We have so much to buy."

"I'd like the students to do some meal planning and prep," Faith said.

"Maybe we can have some special Friday meals. Grill hamburgers and other favorites of the kids," Patrice said. "Perhaps we can recruit some moms to help."

†

Patrice closed her notepad. "My eyes are starting to cross. I think it's time for me to hit the road."

Faith stood and walked out with her. "I'll see you in the morning."

"I'll be here around nine if that's okay?"

"That will be great. Drive safe."

"I will." Patrice drove away, and Faith sat on the steps.

†

Logan waved as Patrice passed the station.

"Are you spending the night at Faith's tonight?" Curtis shot his daughter a grin.

Logan smiled. "I was thinking I might."

"Go then and have some fun. I'll close up and head home. See you tomorrow."

"Thanks, Dad," Logan said as she wiped her hands on a shop towel. She kissed him on the cheek and walked out to her truck. She rarely arrived at Faith's before the sun went down, so she might be surprised to see her so early.

When she turned onto Faith's driveway, she spotted her playing fetch with Finder. She smiled and parked out of the way.

"Finally, a relief pitcher," Faith said as Logan walked toward her.

"Is she wearing you out?"

"She loves playing fetch."

Logan sat beside Faith and leaned over to kiss her. She took the ball and tossed it for Finder. "Did you have a good day? I saw Patrice go by a few minutes ago."

"Yeah, we got a lot done today. Did you have a good day? I'm surprised to see you this early. Pleased, too." Faith placed her hand on Logan's thigh. "Will you stay for dinner tonight?"

"For dessert, too," Logan said. "If that's okay."

"I didn't bake anything today." Faith chuckled.

"You are plenty sweet enough for me."

"Good. I've got no idea what to cook. We've been so busy today I forgot to take anything out to thaw."

"How about some breakfast? French toast or something?"

"That's easy enough."

When they walked inside, once Finder was tired, Logan spun Faith in her arms for a proper kiss. "I've missed you. Oh, here's the payment from last night." She pulled the envelope from her pocket and handed it to Faith.

"Thanks. I had an idea today. I'll start saving a little to create a scholarship fund for any of our kids who might wish to further their education."

"Keep half of my portion then. I really don't need that much for gas or maintenance."

Faith cocked her head at Logan. "Are you serious?"

"Yes. Take it from my portion. You need every cent you can to keep the community stocked. I know you don't keep anything for yourself."

Faith felt her eyes filling with tears at Logan's generosity. She turned to the refrigerator to pull out eggs and milk.

"Do I have time to run through the shower and get some of this funk off me?"

"Go ahead. I won't start cooking until I hear the shower turn off."

"I won't be long." Logan kissed her before leaving the kitchen.

Faith opened the envelope and removed a hundred-dollar bill for Logan. She noticed a note and pulled it out to check it. 'I could quickly sell twice as much if you can provide it. I'm good for more five-gallon buckets. Let me know.'

Doubling the order would be a great way to fund a scholarship account. She would discuss it with Logan to see if it was worth the risk for a larger order. She stood, started preparing the bread's egg bath, and pulled out a frying pan.

CHAPTER SEVEN

The summer months flew by faster than Faith hoped. She and Patrice had successful meetings with their students, and all chose to attend the school. The classrooms were all set up and ready for students. Patrice and Faith were hanging the last decorations in the cafeteria when they heard a vehicle approaching.

"I think our vans have arrived," Patrice told Faith.

"Let's go take a look," Faith said.

They walked outside, and Faith stopped dead in her tracks when she saw the vans. They weren't brand new, but they were in good shape. What caught her off guard was the magnetic sign on the passenger door. Her hands covered her mouth, and tears filled her eyes when she read, "Wilson Church School."

"Did you know?" she asked Patrice.

"No. I didn't have a clue."

"That was my personal touch," Max said as he handed each of them a set of keys. "I know this was your grandpa's church, so I thought it was a fitting name."

"It's perfect," Faith said.

"They have a few miles on them, but they're in good shape. Logan will probably inspect them, but I assure you they are sound."

"Thank you, Max." Faith hugged his neck.

"Thank you both for what you're doing for these kids. I'm proud to have been a part of getting it ready."

"Would you join us for the Open House on Friday?" Faith smiled. "Logan is grilling burgers, and the community is pitching in for side dishes, drinks, and desserts."

"I'd love to. What can I bring?"

"Just an appetite. We should have plenty to eat," Faith told him.

"I hope Miss Ruth will be donating some of her pies. I got addicted to them while we were working out here."

"Several, and her sweet tea, too."

"I'll be here around eleven. I can help if you need an extra set of hands. Enjoy the vans. I'll see you Friday," Max said. He walked over to the third vehicle to ride back to the office.

Patrice watched him drive away and looked at Faith. "I think it's time to call Toby and run the route with him before next week."

"Why don't you stop by on your way home and get him to come out tomorrow?"

"I can do that. Is there anything else we need to do before Friday?"

Faith shrugged. "I'm sure something will come up, but I can't think of anything right now. The rooms are ready, we have plenty of supplies to get started, the internet is up, and our iPads are good to go."

"I'll go to the store tonight and get the burger patties and buns to bring them out tomorrow. Can you think of anything else?"

"If all of our community folks bring what they've signed up for, we'll have enough to feed an army." Faith started walking toward a van. "You'll find this community likes to pitch in and cook. Even if they don't have much, almost everyone contributes something."

"I've kind of gotten that impression. Nobody has said 'no' to any of our requests."

"Even the families that haven't had school-age kids for years." Faith opened the door to one of the vans. "Maybe not new, but better than a stinky old school bus any day."

Patrice had opened the door to the other van. "Amen to that. This one is pretty clean, too."

"Toby is so excited. He asked me if it's starting time every time I see him."

Patrice saw Finder approaching with her ball in her mouth. "I think someone believes it's time to play. I'll lock up and head home."

"Don't worry about locking up. I'll take care of that. Drive safe, and I'll see you tomorrow." Finder placed the ball in her hand, and Faith hurled it as far as she could.

"I wish I had her energy," Patrice said. "Have a great night."

"You, too." Faith walked toward the steps to the church and sat. Finder rushed back to her with the ball, and once Patrice pulled away, Faith tossed it again. She looked at the vans and then toward her grandfather's grave. "I hope you approve. I think it's the perfect name." Faith felt a soft breeze caress her face. Finder had returned and was waiting patiently for Faith. She dropped the ball into Faith's hand.

"You sure are growing," Faith said when Finder tired and sat beside her. "What should we cook for Logan tonight?"

Finder's ears perked at Logan's name. "I know you love her, too." She looked at Finder. "I think it's fried chicken night."

Finder licked her lips.

"No, ma'am. No people food for you." Faith locked up the church and walked to the house. Logan hadn't officially moved in yet, but she was spending more nights with Faith, much to her delight. They had agreed to double the Holy Water order, so they would cook longer than usual on the nights they cooked. Faith knew she was getting spoiled waking up next to Logan. She felt herself smiling as she toiled in the kitchen.

†

Logan entered the house and hugged Faith from behind. "You have got it smelling so good in here. My mouth started watering as soon as I stepped onto the porch."

"I hope you're hungry. I cooked more than I realized."

"I am starved," Logan replied. "Do I have time to shower?"

"Yes. Everything should be ready when you return."

Logan kissed Faith's neck.

"Don't forget to speak to our daughter. You know she gets offended if you ignore her."

Logan knelt down and fussed over Finder, who rushed to her basket, pulled out a ball, and dropped it at Logan's feet. Logan chuckled and looked at Faith.

"Go ahead. I know you want to play as much as Finder does. There's nothing that will get cold."

"Let's go, girl," Logan said as they walked outside.

Faith washed up a few dishes while she waited. She looked out the window and watched Logan and Finder play for several minutes until a timer going off caught her attention.

Logan was laughing when they returned inside. "I'll hurry," she told Faith as she walked down the hallway.

Faith nodded and turned on the coffee pot. It was going to be a late night.

†

Logan started the still while Faith cleaned up the kitchen. It would take some time to get up to the temperature to create the drip, so she went back upstairs. As soon as she reached the root cellar, she could smell the aroma of baking cookies.

"You have perfect timing," Faith said as she placed cookies on a plate to cool and puta second batch in the oven. "Pour the milk; these will cool in just a few minutes."

Logan poured the milk and eyed the cookies. "Don't even think about it. Remember last time you burned your tongue because you couldn't wait." Faith kissed Logan. "I can think of much better uses for your tongue."

"I can most definitely wait for cookies then," Logan replied with a grin. "It's going to be a while before the mash runs if we want to give my tongue a workout."

"Cookies first since you've already poured the milk."

†

Logan took Faith in her arms and kissed her sweetly. "Thank you for baking cookies."

"I know how much you like them. I figured some extra energy wouldn't hurt either of us tonight."

Logan led Faith into the bedroom and removed her shirt and bra. One advantage to being freshly showered was Logan only wore a T-shirt and shorts, so she pulled them off as Faith removed her jeans and panties. Logan sat on the edge of the bed. "Let's see if my tongue is still working." Logan's mouth was at the perfect height to reach Faith's breasts, and she lazily circled each nipple with her tongue. "I believe it still works. Your nipples seem to enjoy the attention."

"Yes, they do," Faith purred.

Logan opened her mouth and covered Faith's left breast, sucking it deeply into her mouth.

"That feels even better," Faith said as she pulled Logan's head closer. She stepped forward and straddled Logan. Logan's hands caressed Faith's back as her mouth tasted her supple breasts. She moved back on the bed to give Faith more support and slipped a hand between them, teasing her opening with the tips of her fingers.

"Oh yes. I want your long fingers deep inside me," Faith urged.

Logan penetrated her and slipped gently deep into her wetness. Faith's muscles contracted around her fingers as her thumb stroked across her swollen clit. Logan curled her fingers inside Faith, and the movement caused Faith to shudder. She slowly withdrew her fingers and then pressed deep, bringing a moan to Faith's lips.

Faith began grinding her hips into Logan's hand as her climax began building.

Logan withdrew her fingers and wrapped Faith in her arms as she turned to lay her on the bed. "I do believe my tongue will feel good right here." Logan's tongue teased Faith's opening until she slipped through the velvety soft entrance. Logan moaned, enjoying the taste and sensation of her tongue as it lapped up her juices. Her fingers reached for Faith's nipples, twisting and gently stretching them, bringing a gasp from Faith.

"Feels so good," Faith said between gasps for breath. She could feel the contractions of her orgasm as they erupted deep within her. "Yes, Logan," Faith cried as she came hard, her body trembling from the intensity for several long moments. Logan tenderly kissed her way up Faith's body until she was stretched out on top of her lover. She could feel the subtle tremors still running through her body. She covered Faith's mouth and shared a long, passionate kiss.

"I'd say it works just fine," Logan said with a chuckle.

"That was incredible," Faith said. "I was long overdue for that."

"It felt magnificent," Logan replied. They cuddled for a short while. "I think I'd better go check to see if we're running yet."

"I'll get dressed and join you in just a minute."

"Take your time. We've got a long night ahead of us." Logan kissed her, slipped into her clothes and shoes, and left the room.

†

Faith lay still for several minutes to relax. When she swung her legs over the side of the bed, they felt like jelly. Faith smiled and opened a drawer to pull out a T-shirt and sweats before stepping into a pair of well-worn loafers. She stopped for a drink of water in the kitchen and looked down to see Finder looking up at her. "Are you ready to go out? I won't be back for a little while."

Finder leaped to her feet and trotted to the door. She stopped to get her ball from the basket and sat down to wait for Faith.

"Okay, I get it. You want to play fetch. Let's go."

Faith and Finder played fetch for ten minutes before returning inside. "I'll take you out again before we go to bed." Finder curled up with her bear and watched Faith disappear into the pantry. Faith locked the door behind her out of habit, then descended the steps into the tunnel. As she neared the cooking room, she could hear the hissing of the still and Logan singing. She had earphones in her ears connected to her phone, so she didn't hear Faith arrive. Logan spun around, moving to the music, and stopped when she saw Faith watching her.

"Hey. I didn't hear you."

"I heard you singing. What was the song? It sounded beautiful."

"It's a new song by Jordan Davis called 'What My World Spins Around.' It reminds me of you."

"Can you play it for me?"

†

Logan placed the headphones in Faith's ears and turned on the song. She watched the smile grow on Faith's face as she listened to the lyrics. Seeing Faith's body sway to the music reminded Logan of how much her world did revolve around her. When the song ended, Faith handed her the earphones.

"I can see why you like it. It's a sweet love song."

"I heard it at the shop on the radio the other day. Dad caught me singing along and said that was our song, and I think he was right. There's some great music coming out, but that just seems to fit."

"I envy your ability to listen to music while you work. When I try to write with music, the words from the songs sneak into my writing."

"It helps the time to pass, especially on slow days. Dad always laughs when I start singing and dancing, but I know he enjoys it, too."

Faith's eyes turned to the still to find a steady drip filling a five-gallon bucket. "Wow, it's cooking up a storm tonight."

"We should finish a second run, about two at this pace."

"I can keep things rolling if you want to catch a nap. Tomorrow will be a long day if you plan to make the drop tomorrow night."

"I'll set my alarm and be back to finish here. When do you want to start doubling the orders?"

"How about next week? We can deliver every week or deliver one big order. What's your preference?"

"I can go either way, but with school starting, we may have to return to cooking on the weekends if we're doing a double batch. One big run would be easier."

"I'll send a note to the buyer that the next delivery will start the doubles then." Faith wrapped her arms around Logan's neck. "Thank you for earlier. Maybe I can return the pleasure when we finish tonight."

"I can wait until Friday night when we can take our time loving one another. I promise it will be worth the wait."

"It always is." Faith kissed her. "Get some sleep."

Faith swapped containers and sat in one of the rockers her grandfather had sat in for years. "I hope you're proud of what we're doing here. I think you would be. You loved this community and its people with all you had."

Faith rocked and listened to the hiss of the still. She knew Toby would be excited about running his route tomorrow. They would stop at each home to introduce him and confirm pick-up and return times with the families. Friday would be a busy day, but she hoped it would be fun for everyone. Faith had sealed up the second bucket and started the second run when Logan returned several hours later.

Logan ran her hand through her hair. "Sorry, I slept through the first alarm."

"That's not a problem. The old girl is cranking the Holy Water out tonight. I just started the first case of jars." She kissed Logan. "Snuggle me when you come back to bed."

"With pleasure. I love you."

"I love you, too."

†

Faith took Finder outside when she emerged from the pantry. The moonless night was dark, but she could still see Finder's movement as she made her rounds. A cool breeze blew the fragrance of mountain laurel, a flowery grape smell. She breathed it deep into her lungs. *It's a shame that something smelling that good is toxic.* She would need to ensure Finder stayed away from the plants in the woods around the house. Finder enjoyed the sound of the crickets until a howl filled the air. Finder turned toward the sound, and her hackles rose along her spine.

95

"It's okay, girl. Just some coyote looking for dinner, but he's a way off. Come on, let's go to bed."

Finder trotted past her and waited for her to lock up before following Faith into the bedroom. Faith left the bathroom light on low, stripped her sweats, and kicked her shoes off before climbing into bed. She snuggled into the pillow Logan had laid her head on and breathed in the scent of her lover. "Good night, Finder." Faith turned out the light and slipped into sweet dreams of Logan.

†

Thursday's practice run went well, and it was difficult to determine who was most excited about school starting on Monday: Toby, the students, Faith, or Patrice. When Patrice left for the day, she looked at Faith. "I'll see you about nine."

"That should be fine. Volunteers will start rolling in around ten, and Logan will fire up the grill for the burgers around eleven."

"I can't remember the last time I was so excited about starting a school year."

"This will be great for all of us," Faith promised.

After Patrice left, Faith opened the door to the tunnel to carry the Holy Water into the room. She wasn't surprised to find that Logan had already moved the buckets and cases of jars. They would get Lightning loaded after they finished dinner and relax until it was time for Logan to make her run. Faith closed the door behind her and started dinner.

†

Logan was about to close up shop for the evening when the sound of the service bell rang. She walked outside to find the state officer who had become a regular customer at the pumps. "It's kind of late for you to be out, isn't it?" Logan teased.

"The captain has decided to set up a license check tonight. He's determined to catch *The Ghost*."

Logan had to chuckle at him, making finger quotes in the air. "What ghost? I know there's plenty of rumors about some haunted sites around here, but nothing too serious."

The officer laughed. "Not that kind of ghost, but it might as well be. Some guy has eluded detection for a long time, so we call him *The Ghost*." He smirked. "No one's ever been close enough to catch a tag or even a vehicle description."

"What's he done to warrant that much interest?"

"Mainly speeding, but it's suspected he's doing something else. Maybe bootlegging or drug transport. He's one hell of a fine driver. Never even taps his brakes; you know how treacherous some of these roads are in daylight."

"Yeah. I can't imagine how terrifying it could be at high speed." Logan finished filling his cruiser and ran his credit card. "Be careful out there tonight," she said, and smiled as she handed him the receipt.

"I will. We'll be lucky to see one or two cars on the highway. If nothing interesting shows up, I'm heading home at one."

"Hey, if you're in the area around lunch, come out to the old Baptist church. A new community school is coming this fall, and we have an open house. Yours truly is grilling the burgers. Stop by, and I'll hook you up with a free lunch."

"I may just do that." He tipped his hat to her and drove off.

97

"That was some interesting information to know," she said as she opened the cash register to place the receipt into the drawer. Logan locked the door behind her and walked to Lightning to head out to Faith's.

†

Faith was sitting on the front porch sipping a cold beer, playing fetch with Finder, when she pulled up. "A cold beer sounds good. Are you ready for another?"

"Not yet," Faith answered.

"Sit tight, and I'll grab one and join you out here. It's turning into a nice evening."

Logan walked inside and smiled at the aroma of lasagna filling the kitchen. She reached into the fridge and pulled out a cold bottle of beer. She returned to sit beside Faith, and Finder rushed to her, wiggling her tail with the ball in her mouth. "Bring it." Finder dropped the ball in her hand and waited for Logan to toss it.

Faith looked at her. "I think she prefers playing with you. Your throwing arm is so much better than mine."

"That's one perk of my job. It keeps me in good shape."

"Are you still planning to make a run tonight?"

"Yes, but I'll need to stick to some back roads."

"Why?"

"One of the state officers has become a regular customer, and he told me they were doing a license check tonight, trying to find *The Ghost*." She took a sip of her beer. "If I take backroads, they should be long gone before I start home. He said they'd probably shut it down at one. He thinks it's a waste of time and doubts they'll see one or two vehicles."

"That was some valuable information. Have you ever considered what your cover story would be if you ever got stopped? You'd need a reason to be on the road that late."

"That's why I keep a box with a carburetor handy. Our town doesn't have an auto parts store, and it could take days to get anything delivered. So, I drove into the city to pick up the part and decided to have dinner and maybe catch a movie. Since I work at a garage, that wouldn't be a stretch. I sometimes make a run for parts, but usually earlier in the day."

"That's reasonably believable. We don't have many options for dinner and none for a movie theater. Even country bumpkins like a good flick now and then."

"That we do. Maybe you will join me one night, and we can do dinner and a movie."

"I'd like that."

Logan tossed the ball. "What's that heavenly smell coming from the kitchen?"

"I got lasagna baking. A salad chilling in the fridge. I just need to toast the bread. Are you hungry?"

"I'm getting there, but I'm enjoying your company. It's so relaxing out here."

"Just let me know when you're ready, and I'll pop the bread into the oven."

"Let me finish my beer," Logan said and took a drink. "It may take me a few minutes to wear Finder out, too."

†

Faith snuggled into Logan's body on the couch as they watched a Braves baseball game. "If they keep playing this good, they'll make it to the playoffs."

"It will be nice to have a team we like to cheer for," Faith replied.

"Amen to that. All they need is three more outs. I'll head out after that."

"Please be extra careful tonight. You got a warning about tonight for a good reason."

Logan buried her face in Faith's neck. "I promise to be extra careful, just for you. I'll try to be quiet when I come in."

"I won't rest easy until I know you're in bed beside me," Faith said.

"Strike out! Hell yeah," Logan cheered, nearly knocking Faith off the couch and causing Finder to rush in to see what was so exciting. "Sorry."

"No need to be sorry. I love seeing your excitement. It's okay, Finder, Mama's just happy."

Finder curled up on the floor next to them and yawned.

"I think she's telling me it's time for bed." Faith laughed. "I'll help you load up and then head to bed."

"That sounds good. We have a big day tomorrow, so you need your rest."

"I'll let you sleep until nine if that's enough for you."

"That should be plenty. I've already moved the grill to the school, and my supplies are also set up."

"Ballgame! Playoffs, here we come."

Faith turned off the television. "Let's get you rolling."

"I'll hand it to you, and then we can carry it out to Lightning."

"Works for me."

When the Holy Water was loaded and secured, Logan took Faith in her arms. "I'll be back before you know it. I love you."

"Love you, too. Please, no chases tonight."

"I will do my best to stay under the radar."

Faith nodded and waited for Lightning to disappear into the night before calling Finder and walking inside. "Be safe," she whispered and closed the front door. She flipped the front porch light on and walked to the bedroom.

†

Logan felt the adrenalin begin coursing through her veins as she pulled out to the highway. She took the first right and headed to a well-worn road she hoped would be safe from detection. Logan couldn't drive as quickly as she usually would on the highway, so she knew the drop would take longer. When she was sure she had passed the location of the planned drop point, Logan turned back to the highway and drove quickly toward the week's planned drop. The destination was farther than usual, so Logan cranked up her music and drove the winding roads with a smile.

When she completed her drop, she stored the envelope in the hidden compartment in her glove box and headed home. She would stick to the highway unless a chase took her off-road. Logan looked at the clock and maintained the speed limit. She could try her story out if the state officers were still at the checkpoint, but she hoped they'd already headed home. Logan was a mile from the turn-off to Faith's when she spotted blue lights approaching rapidly from behind. She eased off the side of the road and let out a deep breath when the cruiser flew past her. Probably going to a car wreck somewhere. Her heart was beating rapidly when she pulled back onto the road and turned on her blinker shortly after. She was happy to make it safely home. Logan removed the envelope, locked the door behind her when she entered the house, placed the envelope on Faith's desk, and crept down the hall to the bathroom. Logan undressed and crawled into the bed. Faith was lying on her side and whispered when she felt Logan's arm wrap around her waist.

"Welcome home. Did I just hear a siren, or was I dreaming?"

"Nope, you weren't dreaming. A state cruiser went screaming past when I was getting ready to turn into your drive. Probably a wreck out on the interstate or something." Logan kissed her neck. "Go back to sleep. I love you."

"Love you, too."

Logan listened to Faith's soft purring sound when she slept, until her body and mind relaxed. She heard a strange noise and leaned over to hear Finder whining in her bed as she dreamed, and her back leg twitched.

CHAPTER EIGHT

Faith sipped a cup of coffee and played with Finder until Patrice arrived. Logan was still sleeping, so she poured them coffee and met Patrice on the porch. "Good morning." She offered Patrice a steaming cup.

"It looks like we will have a beautiful day. Thanks," Patrice said when she took the coffee and sat beside Faith.

"No rain and moderate temperatures. We couldn't have ordered better weather."

Patrice nodded toward Lightning. "Logan still sleeping?"

"Yeah. Logan had a long day yesterday, so I decided to let her sleep in a bit. She rarely gets to do that."

"That's sweet of you. I can't wait to see the students' reaction to the school. We took it beyond our initial plans with the big screen television and table games in the recreation room."

Faith shrugged. "I thought we should take advantage of everything while we could. Some of these kids may not even have a television at home."

"I hadn't thought of that."

Finder curled up in a spot of sunshine breaking through the trees. They finished their coffee, and Faith offered a refill.

"Sure, why not. Let's take it to the school and do a final walk-through. I think we're ready, but fresh eyes might see something."

Faith unlocked the door, and they walked inside. A serving table was set up in the cafeteria and filled with paper plates, utensils, napkins, and cups. The burgers would be placed on the end. The next table would be condiments for the burgers, and the start of two tables with salads and desserts.

"I think we're good here. We can serve drinks from the kitchen."

"I think you've done this once or twice," Patrice teased.

"Sunday dinners on the grounds gave me lots of practice serving a large group."

"I bet. Since you know all about that, why don't you let me handle giving the tours?"

Faith nodded, and they walked through the classrooms. She smiled at the tables set up for the kids and the brand-new iPads they would use for their schoolwork. Pencils, pens, notebooks, and other supplies were arranged for each child. Faith was exceptionally proud of the individualized backpacks that sat in a chair for each student. She was positive they had never received such a good setup for school. Both classrooms had a large bookshelf filled with donated and purchased books for each age group. Patrice had gone to a local mass bookstore and convinced the manager to provide a hefty donation of books. She returned with four large boxes of books. They would provide a lending library, and hopefully, they would continue to grow their reading selections.

They were nearly finished with their walk-through when they heard a noise from outside. Faith opened the door and found Logan filling her grill with charcoal. Logan looked up at their approach, and Faith smiled at the smear of charcoal dust on Logan's cheek. She licked her thumb and tried to brush it away, smearing it even worse. "Oh, damn. I just made it worse."

"No worries. I'll get the fire going and go wash my face. Good morning, Patrice."

"Hey, Logan. I didn't think we'd see you for a while."

"I needed to get the coals started. The first guests will arrive at eleven, right? I wanted to have hot burgers waiting for them."

"She's as excited as we are," Faith replied.

They turned at the sound of an approaching vehicle to find Toby arriving. "Hey, ladies," he said when he stepped out of the car. "Ma wanted me to bring the tea and some cakes and pies to get them set up for you."

"Do you need some help, Toby?" Logan asked.

"I'll never turn down help," he answered.

Logan lit the charcoal and then walked with Toby.

"We can carry the desserts if you bring the tea containers," Faith said.

"Sounds like a deal." Toby grinned. "Ma is closing at noon, so she wants us to save her a plate."

"Dad is closing early to join us, too. Have Miss Ruth call him if she wants a ride," Logan said.

"That's perfect. I can come out earlier to help then." Toby smiled.

105

Faith was energized to see how excited everyone was about the school. Getting it ready had been a total commitment from the community, and she was proud of her friends and neighbors. Toby and Logan carried four large containers of sweet tea and placed them on the kitchen counter.

"I've got a cooler of soda, too," Toby said. "My contribution."

"Thank you, Toby. That is very generous of you," Patrice told him.

Faith saw a bit of color rise on Toby's cheeks. She wondered if it was for the compliment or the fact it came from Patrice? A glance at Logan told Faith she hadn't missed the blush either. "I can't wait to have a bite of this coconut cake. Your mama makes the best."

"I'll be sure to share that with you. Is there anything else we might need?"

Faith thought for a second. "Do you have another cooler, Toby?"

"Yes, ma'am. Sure do. What do you need?"

"Would you raid your mama's ice machine and bring a cooler full when you come? We can never have too much ice."

"You got it. Just call me if there's anything else."

"We will, Toby. Thank you for everything."

"My pleasure. I'll see you in an hour or so."

They watched Toby drive off, and then Logan turned to Faith. "I'm going to get my table and utensils set up to cook. Can I steal a couple of the large pans from the kitchen to put the cooked burgers in and some aluminum foil?"

"I'll bring them out for you. Is there anything else you need?"

"I think I'm good. I'll get the burgers going as soon as the coals are ready. Wait, can I borrow a folding chair from the rec room?"

"Like you even have to ask. I'll carry a couple out for you," Patrice said. "I know how an open grill attracts men."

"That it does. I'll have more help than I need in an hour or so." Logan smiled. "I think everyone is excited for today. This is probably our largest event since your grandpa passed."

"He will definitely be smiling down on us today," Faith said.

"He would be proud." Logan smiled at Faith. "I better wash my face before I get some ribbing from the townspeople."

†

Logan had placed the first batch of burgers on the grill when she heard a noise and turned to see a line of cars coming down the driveway. The sight made her heart fill with pride. "Faith. You and Patrice need to come to see this," she called into the school.

Faith and Patrice rushed through the side door to see cars start to fill the parking lot. At the head of the line was Max from the school district. He got out, picked up a large box, handed it to another man, and then picked up another. When he approached, he smiled at Faith and Patrice. "I hope you don't mind me bringing the old man with me." Max chuckled. "You know it's hard to pass on a free meal."

"Hello, Superintendent," Patrice said. "This is Faith Wilson, and this is our school. Welcome. Please come inside, and I'll give you a tour."

"We told you to bring an appetite, but it looks like you got much more," Faith teased Max.

"What's an excellent open house without a housewarming gift? I bought you an ice cream maker and supplies to last a while. I thought it would be a fun learning task for the kids, and who doesn't love ice cream? I need to get this plugged in before this batch turns to mush. I hope everyone likes strawberry ice cream."

"That sounds delicious, and it's a lovely gift. Let's take it to the cafeteria and get it plugged in."

Faith and Max followed Patrice and the superintendent inside. "Hey, Miss Betsy," Faith called out to an older woman who was always a godsend when the church held special events. "Just like old times. Will you coordinate the dishes as they arrive? There's room in the fridge for anything that needs to chill. The oven is turned on warm. I hope those are your famous baked beans."

The jovial Miss Betsy smiled at Faith. "I know how much you like them. I'll stick them in the oven. Are the aprons still behind the door?"

Faith nodded. "Don'tcha know it. Thanks for helping out."

"My pleasure. Your grandpa would be proud of what you're doing here."

"I think so, too. If you've got this, I'll help the others as they come in."

"I can help carry dishes, too," Max offered. "That way, I get a good preview of all the goodies." Max winked at Faith.

"Good point. Let's go see who needs our help."

Toby had pulled up next to the church, and Max helped him carry a large ice cooler into the kitchen. Toby smiled at Miss Betsy. "Will this be out of your way by the counter?"

"That will be perfect, Toby. Thank you."

Miss Betsy opened a drawer and smiled when she saw a pad of post-it notes and a marker. She took them to the table to identify the dishes' owners. From years of experience, she knew how protective the community's women could get over their cookware.

Faith saw her and smiled. "I knew I was forgetting something."

"The good Lord knows we can't misidentify anyone's CorningWare," Miss Betsy said with a wink.

"Amen." Faith chuckled. "The fastest way I know to start a brawl."

"Seriously?" Max asked.

"Sir, do not mess with a country woman's dishes if you know what's good for you. So be careful you don't drop anything," Miss Betsy warned.

Max gently handed a casserole dish to Miss Betsy to label. "Maybe I should go see if Logan needs any help. There's not much I can break there."

"Go ahead. We've got this. Thank you for the ice cream maker," Faith told him.

"My pleasure. It's the least I can do for you."

†

The students were super excited to see their classrooms and all the fun plans posted on their first month of school calendars.

"I can't wait for Monday." Faith heard Sadie Morgan tell her mother. It felt good to listen to the excitement in their voices.

"I usually have to drag my kids out of the house to meet the bus," one mother told her. "They are so happy to be coming to school here. I think they will actually learn something beneficial here."

"We will go beyond traditional academics to help prepare them for adult life," Patrice told her. "There are many common skills schools fail to teach kids these days. We want to provide every opportunity for every student to be successful."

"We've needed this school for years. Thank you both for realizing that," the superintendent said when he heard the mother's comment.

Faith pointed to Patrice. "It was all her idea."

"My idea, but it couldn't be possible if you hadn't agreed to use the church and co-teach. We make a good team."

"I have to agree with that," he said. "Very impressive setup, ladies. Let me know what your other needs may be once school starts."

"We sure will," Patrice assured him.

"Who's ready for burgers?" Max asked as he carried the first pan of burgers into the cafeteria.

"Before we start to eat, I'd like to ask Miss Betsy to bless this meal for us," Faith said.

Miss Betsy pushed a fallen strand of hair from her face. "Please bow your heads. Dear Lord, thank you for the bountiful feast we are about to share, but most importantly, thank you to Faith and Patrice for making all of this possible. This community has needed a school for years. Through their hard work and the support from the community, the dream is about to come true. Bless the food and everyone in the room for a great school year. Amen."

"Thank you. Dig in, folks." Faith smiled when a line formed to receive the heartfelt meal.

Logan was sweating over the grill removing the last of the burgers when the state police cruiser pulled up beside the church.

She smiled when the man stepped out of the vehicle. "I was beginning to wonder if you'd show up today."

"It's been a busy morning out on the interstate. It took me a while to get away. You sure got it smelling good."

"Hang on for a second, and I'll take you inside for some food."

"May I help?"

"You can carry the pan of burgers in for me." Logan closed the lid on the grill.

Cal carried the pan inside, and when Logan saw Miss Betsy, she called out. "Miss Betsy, this is my friend, Cal Burns. Will you see he gets plenty to eat?"

"Come with me, young man, and we'll get you all taken care of." She smiled at Cal.

Cal smiled at being called a young man since he was in his early thirties, but he followed Miss Betsy like a puppy.

Logan looked around to see Faith talking with the school's superintendent and decided to grab something cool to drink, and then she'd fix her a plate of food. Miss Betsy got Cal set up, and he joined her. Logan wiped her brow and smiled up at Miss Betsy.

"Now, what can I get you? You've been working your tail off all day. What do you like on your burgers? I assume you want a bit of everything else."

"Thanks, Miss Betsy, but I'll get a plate in a minute."

"Nonsense. I'll make one up for you."

"Any of Miss Ruth's coconut cake left? Plenty of your baked beans, too."

"You got it," Miss Betsy answered. "I'll be right back."

"So, what's the story here?" Cal asked.

"Faith's grandfather was the preacher here for years, but they couldn't find another preacher after his death, so the church has been vacant for a few years. She used to teach school and was

111

approached by Patrice Long about using the school and team teaching with her. There are fourteen school-aged kids in our community that ride a bus for over an hour each way to school, and the school environment in the city isn't pleasant for country kids."

"I can imagine," Cal said between bites. "That's a great idea."

"Most kids from this area, including me, drop out as soon as they turn sixteen due to the bullying and lack of attention in classes. Faith was one of the smart ones who made it through college and came back here when her grandfather fell ill."

"You seem to be doing pretty well for yourself. I hear you're one of the area's best mechanics."

"My dad is an excellent teacher, and I will take over the business when he retires. I will teach a class here on Fridays on simple automotive maintenance, and I hope to get a kid interested in being an apprentice."

"That's a win-win situation, and these kids need basic skills. I don't know how many kids I see stranded on the road when they can't change a tire or run out of gas."

"Exactly. That's why I want to teach the students some of the basics. Checking fluids, changing oil, rotating tires. The stuff they can do for little to no cost."

Cal looked at her. "Do you think I could come by and teach a session on road safety and law enforcement?"

"That's a wonderful suggestion. I'll introduce you to Patrice and Faith before you leave, and you can make the suggestion. I bet they'd love the idea."

Miss Betsy returned with a plate mounded with food and placed it in front of Logan.

"How many people did you expect to eat off this plate, Miss Betsy?"

"Just you. You're getting too skinny." Miss Betsy laughed. "There wasn't a massive slice of cake left, so I loaded you up with casseroles."

"Thank you, Miss Betsy. It's going to take hours to eat all this."

"There's no rush. Most of the guests have gone, and we can start the cleanup while you relax and eat."

"Have Faith and Patrice eaten yet?"

"No, but they are next on my radar as soon as they finish talking with that feller."

"Thank you, Miss Betsy. You're my hero."

When Max and the superintendent left, Miss Betsy waved them over. "Sit, and I will fix your plates. You two haven't stopped long enough to eat anything."

"Have you eaten, Miss Betsy?"

"Faith, you should know by now I nibble while I work. I'll make your plates and share some tea with you."

"Faith and Patrice, this is my friend Cal Burns. He's got an idea to share with you."

"Nice to meet you ladies. Logan was telling me about the school, and I was wondering if I could come in one day to talk about road safety and law enforcement?"

"I love it," Patrice said and clapped her hands together. "I'll teach the older group, and I'm sure they could benefit from that."

"I have the little ones, and while they aren't ready for road safety, I'm sure they would find you interesting to talk to." Faith smiled at Cal. "Just let us know when you are available, and we'll work you into the class schedule."

113

"Thank you. I will get my boss to approve some dates, and we can go from there." Cal was beaming with pride. "I am impressed by what you have going here. It's a much-needed service from what I can tell."

"We hope to make a difference and maybe help one or two students achieve a college education," Faith replied. "We've been planning a way to start a scholarship fund."

"Please let me know when you do. I'd gladly donate towards that," Cal answered. The radio on his shoulder squawked with an emergency call. "I'm sorry, I have to eat and run. Thanks for a great lunch, and good luck."

"Be safe, Cal," Logan called after him.

†

When the feast was done and all items cleaned and stored, Patrice, Logan, and Faith sat in the cafeteria sipping tea. "What a great event. I think it was a success," Faith said.

"Everyone seemed to have a great time and a good meal. I don't think anyone went away hungry," Logan said. "It felt good to send some leftovers home, so the families could have another good meal."

"Some kids ate like they were bottomless pits," Patrice said.

Faith looked at Logan. "Many families don't have much, so I'm sure the children hadn't seen this much food in one place in a long time."

"If ever," Logan added. "Especially the desserts." She took a sip of tea to hide her emotion. "The next time we go to town, I'm going to buy several boxes of brownie and cake mixes you can use in your cooking classes."

"I think Max brought enough supplies to make ice cream every week for at least a year."

"That ice cream maker is a dream. Do you remember when we had to take turns sitting on the lid and turning the crank for hours?" Logan asked Faith.

"I do. Those were great times and made us appreciate the end product because we had to work for it," Faith said.

"Today was a great reminder of how much I took for granted being raised in the city," Patrice admitted. "If I wanted ice cream, I just went to the freezer or waited for the ice cream truck to come through the neighborhood. It really hit home, the living conditions of the families here." Patrice wiped at her eyes. "I know there is no shortage of love, but my heart ached for some kids today."

"That should only confirm that we are doing the right thing here. I was shocked to see Mary Beth Hudson. She's maybe eighteen, had one kid on her hip, and is pregnant with another." Faith sighed deeply.

Logan placed a hand on her shoulder. "Close. She was sixteen when she got pregnant and dropped out last year. The father is nowhere in the picture. Some older kid she met at school, but he won't man up and do what's right by her or the kids."

"Has anything been done to get a social worker on her case? They can do some paternity testing and make the man at least pay child support," Patrice suggested.

"I don't know," Logan said. "If anyone would know, it would be Miss Ruth. I swear she sees and hears everything in this community."

"If you can find out and let me know, I'll contact social services to see what can be done."

Logan nodded. "Thanks, Patrice. She's not the first girl to be taken advantage of by a city boy, but hopefully, she'll be the last."

"I think I will head home if we're done here. It's been a long day." Patrice stood to leave. "Monday is the real deal, so rest up." She grinned at them. "Thanks for making this day so successful."

"Don't forget your to-go box. Hang on, and I'll get them for us," Logan said.

Faith flipped off the lights and locked the door behind her. She walked Patrice to her car. "I guess I'll see you bright and early Monday."

"Have a good weekend. I hope you both get some rest." Patrice entered her car and put her box on the seat next to her.

"You, too. Drive carefully."

As they walked to the house, Logan draped an arm around Faith's shoulders. Finder was sound asleep on the front porch. "I think the kids finally wore her out," Faith said.

"They were playing hard. It was tough to tell who was having the most fun, the kids or the dog."

"I need a hot shower. Will you join me?"

"You don't appreciate my burger smoke perfume?" Logan grinned.

"You smell delicious, but I think we will enjoy a shower."

"Let me put this food away. What about Finder?" Logan asked.

"Let her sleep. I'll leave the screen door cracked open. She can come in that way if she wakes."

†

Logan took her leisure, bathing Faith's body as they made love in the shower. The cooling of the water was the incentive for leaving the bathroom to continue in the bedroom. They made love and snuggled for hours.

"It feels good to not be rushed," Logan admitted.

"I know you worry about your dad, but have you given more consideration to moving in with me? You are out here quite often."

"Honestly, I have, and I believe I'm getting more confident with Dad living alone. Just give me a few more weeks."

"Sweetheart, you can take all the time you need. I enjoy waking up next to you, and I will be satisfied with however often we get the privilege. Don't rush on my account. Do what's right for you and your dad."

"I promise it won't be much longer. I look forward to waking up with you every day, too."

Finder placed her head on the edge of the bed and whined.

"I think our daughter is telling us she's hungry and wants to be fed." Faith chuckled. "She did work up an appetite playing with the kids today."

"She was great with them. Little Sadie was tearful when they left until her mom told her she'd see her next week. She ran back to Finder, hugged her neck, and told her, 'I'll see you soon.' She loved the kiss Finder placed on her cheek, too."

Faith's hand stroked the dog's head. "She is such a good girl. I'll be up in a minute to feed you." She looked at Logan. "What would you like to eat?"

"We have plenty of leftovers from today. Could I convince you to fry an egg I can put on my burger?"

"That does sound good. If you start warming up the hot foods in the microwave, I'll feed Finder and then fry some eggs."

"Deal." Logan rolled out of bed and dressed. "Would you like to spend a relaxing night on the couch? Maybe see if there's a good movie playing?"

"That sounds like a great way to end a perfect day," Faith said as she slipped a T-shirt over her head.

CHAPTER NINE

The first few weeks of school proceeded beautifully as the students learned the new routines. Faith and Patrice analyzed the strengths and weaknesses to better understand each child's needs. As they had expected, the children lagged behind in reading and math. Logan started her automotive class and was in heaven teaching the kids new skills.

All was going smoothly until Logan came out one night to deliver some supplies. She had made a run to town for parts and stopped by to pick up the brownie and cake mixes she had promised Faith.

Logan found Faith crying as she sat at the kitchen table. The redness in her eyes and the tear stains on her cheeks made Logan's heart ache. She knelt down beside Faith and brushed away her tears. "What's wrong?"

"Sadie came to school this morning with a large bruise on her arm. When I asked her how she got it, she shrugged, but it looked like finger marks where someone grabbed her. I could see the look of concern in her eyes that I would press her for an answer."

"Is this the first time you've seen anything like that?"

"Yes, it is. I know that as an educator, I am a mandatory reporter, but I don't want to jump the gun if this was a simple accident."

"This is a new school with a totally new environment. Sadie has to learn she can trust you. I'm sure that's been an issue for her, especially at a young age. Give her time to get to know you, and if there's something not kosher going on, maybe she will open up to you."

"I hope it was just a minor thing like catching her to break a fall or something, but deep in my gut, I don't believe that is what happened."

"Have you considered talking to her mother to see if there was an accident?"

"No, not yet. That should be my next step since Sadie won't tell me."

"Have you discussed this with Patrice? Sadie has an older brother in her class, right?"

"Yes. Chuck, he's thirteen."

"Maybe see if she has seen any bruises on him or if he knows what happened to Sadie's arm."

Faith forced a smile and nodded. "That's a good idea. I can't be jumping to conclusions."

"There may be a simple explanation," Logan said.

"I hope so," Faith responded, but Logan knew she didn't believe it for a minute.

"I know we've made some deliveries to her home, but I've never seen her dad. What do you know of him?"

"Only that his name is Jerry, according to Sadie's school profile. I've never met him either."

"I'll check with Dad to see if he knows him and get the down-low if there is any. If anyone here will know, it's Curtis." Logan smiled and stood next to Faith. She reached for her hand. "Come on. We're getting out of here."

"What? I haven't eaten or anything yet."

"Good, we'll find something to eat in the city. You need some wind in your hair to ease your mind."

Faith shook her head, but she knew once Logan made her mind up to do something, there was no way she could stop her. She stood and kissed Logan. "I can't stay out late. I've got school to teach tomorrow."

"I promise to have you home by ten. Ten thirty at the latest."

†

Logan was right. The wind blowing through her hair made her feel better. Or at least it pushed her thoughts to the back of her mind for a while. She held her hand out the window and let her hand surf the winds as Logan drove the country roads with expertise. Logan's radio blared country music as she drove.

Logan glanced over at Faith, and the smile on her face warmed her heart. The distress she was experiencing earlier now appeared to be the last thing on her mind. She was glad Faith was distracted when they passed the Morgan home.

As they neared the city, she turned down the radio and broke the silence between them. "What do you feel like eating?"

"Sushi," Faith answered and laughed at the way Logan's face wrinkled in disgust.

"I don't know why anyone would eat fish bait," Logan teased.

"They have several options that are fully cooked. Where's your sense of adventure?"

"Sitting right next to me."

"Try it. You might like it. You can order a Hibachi dinner if you don't like the sushi I order for you."

Logan was trapped. There was no way she could turn down Faith's suggestions. She sighed. "Where am I going?"

"Take a right at the second intersection," Faith answered and slid close to Logan. "It's been ages since I've had sushi."

Logan smiled at her as she approached the intersection and turned on her blinker. "We are about to remedy that."

Faith gave her directions to the restaurant and convinced Logan to try a surf-and-turf sushi roll. She watched Logan's eyebrows lift when she took her first bite.

"That's not half bad."

"The green paste-like stuff is wasabi and is extremely spicy, so go easy with it. It will definitely open up your sinuses."

"Other parts, too, I'm sure." Logan chuckled. "You can have all of that other stuff."

"That's ginger, and I like it, so you eat all the wasabi you want."

"Deal." Logan scooped up a tiny bit of wasabi and placed it on the sushi before lifting it to her mouth. "It's going to take more than one to fill me up."

"Do you want another roll or something from the grill?"

"How about another one of these and some fried rice?" Logan asked.

"That's easy enough." Faith caught the attention of the server and ordered the food. "So, another sushi fan?"

Logan shrugged. "I guess I can be convinced. I'm still not ready for anything raw, or that I'd put on the end of a fish hook."

"That's fair enough. I promise I won't order anything raw for you."

The second roll would have been enough to fill Logan up, but she took several bites of the fried rice and had the rest boxed to take home. "That was delicious." She paid the bill and walked outside. "Is there anything you need while we're in town?"

"I believe I'm good. Thank you for dinner. It was as good as I remember it."

"My pleasure, ma'am," Logan said and opened the door for Faith. "Home?"

Faith nodded and slid across the seat toward Logan. Logan draped an arm around Faith's shoulders and held her close. She could feel Faith's hand on her thigh, and her touch made Logan tingly all over. She looked over at Faith five minutes later and smiled. Faith had fallen asleep on her shoulder.

The new Jordan Davis song, "What My World Spins Around" began playing on the radio. *That is so how I feel about her.* Logan listened even closer to the lyrics. *Perfect.*

†

Faith was startled awake when Logan turned onto her drive. She sat up straight and wiped her face. "I'm sorry I fell asleep on you."

"I enjoyed every minute of it. You've been working hard lately."

"Still, that's no excuse. Thanks for a great meal."

"It was a good break for both of us. I'm going to make a run tomorrow night, so I'll see you then," Logan said. She parked and turned to Faith.

"Do you want some company?"

"Want, yes, but you have to be up early these days for school. Maybe you can ride along the next time I make a weekend run."

"You have to be up early, too."

"Naw, Dad will cover the station until I get there. We don't have much mechanical work this week." Logan kissed Faith and stepped out to offer her a hand out of the truck. "I'll see you tomorrow night."

"Thank you for everything, Logan."

Logan nodded shyly and then watched Faith walk into the house before she climbed inside Lightning. When she reached the paved road, she floored the gas pedal and felt the truck lurch forward powerfully. It felt good, and she sighed when the front porch light of her home came into view all too soon.

†

Logan was surprised to find her dad still awake and reading at the kitchen table. "You're up late," she told him as she walked in and turned out the porch light.

"Just doing some reading. Did you have a good night?"

"Yes. Faith and I drove to the city for dinner. We both needed a break."

Curtis wrinkled up his face. "Something wrong?"

"I'm not sure, Dad. Faith was upset today that one of her students came to school with a suspicious bruise. I suggested a ride to clear her head." Logan sat next to him. "Do you know Jerry Morgan?" Logan could see the flash of recognition in his eyes.

"Is he the dad?"

"Yes, he has two kids attending the school."

Curtis shook his head. "Jerry is an angry man. Has been for years. He was a star athlete. Probably the best to come out of this little town. He was on a path to a college scholarship for football. Then his dad died."

"That sucks," Logan said.

"He was called home to work the family farm, which he kept until his ma passed five years later, but his time as an athlete had passed. He's been an angry man since the day his dad died. It ruined all the plans to make it to the NFL one day, and he could have made it with hard work." Curtis took a drink of water. "Once his ma passed, he sold the acreage to a neighbor and vowed to never be a sharecropper again."

"So, what did he do?"

"He couldn't afford to move away, so he took a job driving a dump truck for a road crew. He made good money until he fell into the bottle and lost his job, further intensifying his anger."

"What does he do now?"

"The last I knew, he was driving a truck, gone for several days at a time, but that's been a year or so. He never comes into town when he's home. If he even bothers to come home anymore."

"He's got a wife and two kids to support," Logan said with a growl in her voice.

Curtis shrugged. "Jerry isn't the type to think of others before his own needs. I don't think Teresa could make it if he wasn't giving her some support, but not what they deserve."

Logan swallowed and asked the difficult question she wanted when the conversation started. "Has he been known to abuse her or the kids?"

"I can't say for sure, but I wouldn't be surprised. Teresa used to do some work for Miss Ruth, but she wouldn't show up for days when he was around. Probably to hide the evidence of his anger, but like I said, I've got no proof." He looked at her. "Faith's grandfather always made sure they had goods. I think Teresa had talked to him on occasion."

Logan smiled. "That sounds like him."

"He can be dangerous, so don't get into his business if you don't have to. If he abuses Teresa, she has support options but must make the first move."

"If it were only that easy, Dad. If his violence and anger are bleeding over onto the kids, something needs to be done."

"A job for law enforcement. Not a vigilante," Curtis warned.

"Do you have faith that something would be done?"

"If there is evidence of child abuse, they could press charges. It's unfortunate that if it's between Jerry and Teresa, it's up to her to press charges. If she's a battered wife, she's probably too terrified. She could also face charges of child endangerment if he abuses them. She would risk losing her children. The foster system is not where any child should end up, but many do."

The information her dad shared with her made her more concerned. She would keep the information close to her chest until Faith could talk to Patrice and maybe Teresa. Logan looked at her dad. "Thanks for sharing that with me."

Curtis nodded, and Logan climbed the stairs to her room, her anger rising with each step she climbed. *How could any man treat his wife and kids like that?*

Logan prepared for bed but tossed and turned for hours. Around three, she bolted upright in her bed from a dream. Sadie's bright blue eyes were filled with tears, and blood ran down her face. "Fuck," Logan growled in the dark room. She lay there for several minutes, unable to get back to sleep. Logan showered, dressed for work, and slipped quietly down the stairs to keep from waking her father.

†

Logan drove to the Morgan house and found a concealed spot to park and watch the house. The place was dark, with no signs of movement. Parked in the drive was a beat-up truck she hadn't seen parked there when she and Faith made their deliveries. Could it be Jerry, she wondered? Logan kept an eye on the house for an hour before a light came on around five o'clock, and thirty minutes later, a dark figure skulked out of the house. She could hear the screen door slam behind him as he stormed toward the truck. His tires squealed with anger as he put the truck in reverse, backed out of the drive into the road, and peeled away down the highway.

She watched with curiosity as the light came on in the kitchen, and she could see movement within. Logan stepped out of Lightning and raced across the yard toward the house. She looked through the kitchen window to find Teresa sitting at the table with her face in her hands. A timer sounded on the stove, and Teresa stood and turned toward the window. Logan could see the swelling of her eyes and a faint bruise through the makeup Teresa had used trying to hide the abuse.

What she did next surprised her. Logan walked to the front door and knocked softly. When Teresa cautiously opened the door, she looked around to ensure Jerry was nowhere in sight.

"We need to talk," Logan said and stepped past Teresa into the house.

"Wh…what about?" Teresa said.

"About this," Logan replied and pointed to her eye. "Even through the makeup, I can see the bruise and swelling."

127

"I was clumsy and slipped in the kitchen."

"I call bullshit, Teresa. What he does to you is between you and God, but when he starts leaving bruises on the kids, it's time for action."

Teresa collapsed in her arms, shedding tears she had fought so hard to control. Logan could feel the dampness on her shirt. "He doesn't mean to hurt us. He's just so angry."

"Don't make an excuse for him, Teresa. It will only continue to get worse. How long has this been going on?"

"For a few years. Rarely at first, until he started drinking. Then he would get lost in the whiskey and lose his love for everyone. He'd curse his parents, me, the children, and everyone he thought ruined his life. I know he loves us, but he can't control himself."

Logan bit her tongue. It would be easy to condemn Jerry and Teresa for not doing right by their family. Instead, she asked, "Has he ever sought help for his drinking?"

"I've suggested it many times, but he refuses to admit he has a problem. He can control his drinking sometimes, but we get the worst of him when it gets the better of him."

"Did he put that bruise on Sadie's arm?"

Teresa broke into tears again. "Yes, he grabbed her when she didn't move fast enough to get him a beer. How did you know?"

"Faith saw it at school yesterday, but Sadie didn't remember how she got it."

"That's the first time he's ever hurt her. Chuck has suffered several whippings for imaginary acts against the father he used to adore. I can feel his anger building toward his dad for the way he mistreats us."

"It's time to break the cycle. I don't have a clue, but something must be done before someone gets seriously hurt or worse. When do you expect him home?"

"Not for two more days. I don't know what to do, Logan. I have very few options."

"But you do have more than you know. Give me time to think and see what I can find out."

They were interrupted by Chuck, who walked into the kitchen. "Hey, Logan, what are you doing here?"

"I saw your light on, and I wanted to tell your mom how good you are doing in the mechanics class."

Chuck's eyes lit with pride. "Do you really think so?"

"I do. I have been impressed with your skills and eagerness to learn. Patrice says you're doing well in your schoolwork, too."

"Reading is still hard." He grinned.

"You just have to keep reading. I think Dad's got some books you might enjoy. Will you read them if I loan you some?"

"Heck yeah. Are any of them westerns? I love westerns."

Logan laughed. "It must be a boy thing. Yes, he has several. I'll bring some out on Friday for our next class."

"Cool," Chuck said. He looked at his mom. "I heard you talking and came down to see that you were okay. I'm going to get showered and ready for school."

"Wake your sister, too. The van will be here before you know it. Do you want something to eat?"

"No, ma'am. Ms. Faith is making biscuits and gravy this morning. They are awesome."

"Oh really? Maybe I should change my class schedule," Logan said.

"I'll cook you breakfast if you stay," Teresa offered.

129

"I hear Miss Ruth's café calling my name. You get these babies ready for school. I'll talk to you later."

Teresa nodded. "Thanks, Logan."

Logan nodded and left the house. As she walked back toward Lightning, she looked up at the sky. "What now, preacher man?" Faith's grandfather would have some advice, but he wasn't here to offer it to her. She climbed into the truck and drove to Miss Ruth's for breakfast and half a pot of coffee. It would be a long day without sleep, but she had promised a customer a delivery tonight. Maybe she'd catch a power nap before going to Faith's.

She walked into the café and smiled. "I want half a pound of that bacon, six eggs, and half a loaf of toast. It smells great in here."

"You're up early. I never see you this early for breakfast," Miss Ruth said.

"Couldn't sleep. Went for a drive and worked up an appetite."

"How many eggs, and how do you want them cooked?" Miss Ruth asked as she filled Logan's cup with coffee.

"Three, over easy, please. Do you have hash browns this morning?"

"I sho nuff do." Miss Ruth chuckled.

†

Curtis was in the garage when she arrived. "You were gone early this morning."

"Couldn't sleep, so I went for a ride and hit Miss Ruth's for breakfast. Did you eat? If not, I'll gladly give these biscuits and gravy a shot." She held up a bag with his breakfast.

"Don't even think about it. I had coffee and toast, but I'm suddenly hungry now that I see that bag. What kept you up last night?"

"Our conversation about Jerry. I had a nightmare about little Sadie and couldn't get back to sleep."

"I see," Curtis said as he opened the bag.

"He was home last night and did a number on Teresa. No makeup could hide that shiner or the swelling. She confirmed he grabbed Sadie, causing the bruise."

"So, you talked to her?"

"Yes, after he left. He won't be back for two days. Do you have any thoughts on what Teresa should do?"

"Let me think about it today. You have a run to make tonight, right?"

"Yes, I do."

"I want you to go home at lunch and get some sleep. I don't need you to fall asleep and end up in a ditch. You need to be rested and alert if you get in a chase. I know you've been smart about varying your schedule, but even the county boys get lucky now and then."

Logan knew his assessment was spot on, and arguing would be a waste of breath. "Yes, sir. Unless we get busy."

"I don't think we'll get a huge rush today." Curtis grinned and shoveled a bite of food into his mouth. "Damn, these are good."

The gas service bell rang, and Logan walked out to see Patrice. "Good morning. Fill her up?"

"Yes, please. I wanted to say how much I appreciate you teaching a Friday class. The students seem to enjoy the lessons."

Logan placed the nozzle in her gas tank and began filling her car. "Several of them are interested in learning. Chuck Morgan picks up on instruction really well."

"He's doing good in most areas, but his reading is slightly behind what it should be."

"I'm going to loan him a few of Dad's books to practice."

"That's a brilliant idea. Could you teach the class how to do an oil change this week on my car? I'll buy whatever supplies you need."

"That could be arranged. Twenty dollars should cover the supplies. I'll give them to you at our cost."

"If I had to buy them elsewhere, what would they cost me?"

"At least thirty," Logan said and ran her fingers through her hair.

"Charge me thirty then. I'm still saving money." Patrice handed her a credit card when the pump stopped. "Go ahead and charge it today if you would."

"No problem. I'll be right back," Logan said. She handed Patrice her card and a receipt to sign when she returned. "Thanks. I'll see you Friday."

"Thank you."

†

She walked back into the garage. "I know she can find gas cheaper in the city, but I'm thankful for her business." Logan started pulling the supplies she'd need for the oil change.

"Amen to that. What's that for?"

"She wants me to teach the kids how to do an oil change on her car."

"Do you want to take the safety ramps or bring them here to learn?"

"Hmmm, a field trip could be fun. I'll ask Faith about it tonight."

"You could tour the garage and teach them about some of the tools we use. See if Patrice needs her tires rotated. I bet they'd love the impact wrench."

"Great idea."

"Your old man comes up with a winner every now and then." Curtis smiled and dropped the trash into the bin.

†

The morning rolled by quickly as Logan struggled to stay busy. She called Faith to discuss a field trip for the students to come to the shop. It would be much easier to work from there. Faith was tickled with the idea and would inform Patrice of the plans.

"Why don't I grab us some lunch, and you can head home for some sleep? We haven't had a customer in the last hour, and I don't see the afternoon being any different."

"That works for me, Dad."

"A club and fries sound good?"

"Absolutely perfect."

"I'll be back in a bit then."

Logan added a few more cases of oil to the shelves and wandered about the shop. She loved the idea of a field trip and was almost sure Patrice and Faith would, too. Thinking about Faith brought a smile to her face, and Logan was deep in thought when she heard the service bell ring. She walked out to find a state officer at the pumps.

"What can I get you today?"

"Can you fill her up and check my fluids? She seems to be running a bit sluggish today," the officer complained.

Logan looked at him. "Slow to get moving?"

"Yeah."

"I can add a fuel additive to clean out her lines. That might help perk her up a bit. If not, I'd recommend you take her to the shop for a tune-up."

"Let's try the additive first. I hate those damn loaner cruisers they give us. I might as well try to chase down a speeder on foot." He chuckled.

Logan added the fuel supplement and pumped his gas. "You might not feel a difference until you're about halfway into the tank. It takes some time to clean the lines, especially if you don't do it every four to five fill-ups, at least with her age. Will you pop the hood?"

The officer reached down and pulled the lever to release the hood latch. "How did you learn so much about cars?"

Logan looked up and nodded toward her dad returning from Miss Ruth's. "I had the world's best teacher." She pulled out the dipstick. "You're not quite a quart low yet, but it looks ready for a change, so I won't add any."

"How long would it take to change?"

"Maybe a half an hour," Logan said.

"Could you do it later today? After your lunch, of course," he said and smiled at Curtis.

"I can do it. Logan's off duty as soon as we finish eating," Curtis replied.

"I'll go pay Miss Ruth a visit for some lunch and come back later." He handed Logan a credit card.

"I'll be right back."

The trooper lifted his hat and ran a hand through his hair. "I have to admit, I've never seen a prettier grease monkey."

"She's a damn fine mechanic," Curtis said and puffed out his chest. "She's far surpassed my skills."

"Here you go," Logan gave him a receipt to sign. "Enjoy your lunch, and thanks for your business."

"My pleasure, ma'am. I'll see you in a bit," he told Curtis and drove away.

"Let's eat," Curtis said.

"What's your choice of drink today, Dad?"

"I think I'll have an RC Cola." He chuckled. "I need to get us a rack of moon pies to sell."

"There's never been a better combination. In my humble opinion." Logan smiled.

"Yours and thousands of other folks. You can't go wrong with that. I think our biggest worry would be keeping me out of them."

"Maybe so." Logan bit into her sandwich.

†

Logan showered and selected an outfit for later before climbing into bed. It hadn't been a busy day, but the lack of sleep was wearing on her. She had barely laid her head on the pillow before being out like a light.

†

Toby had all the kids loaded in the van for the ride home when Faith looked at Patrice. "I could use a coffee."

"Or something stronger." Patrice laughed.

"Do you have some time for coffee? I'd like to get your advice on something."

"Sure. Go get the coffee brewing, and I'll lock up here."

135

Faith started a pot, pulled out two cups, and placed them on the counter. When she heard Patrice's steps on the porch, she called, "Come on in."

"You have a serious look on your face. Is everything okay?"

"I'm concerned with Sadie Morgan. I think she may be being abused at home. She had a large handprint bruise on her arm yesterday. When I questioned her, she claimed she didn't know how she got the bruise." Faith took a sip of coffee. "Have you noticed anything with Chuck?"

Patrice shook her head. "Nothing like a physical mark, but he appears very hand-shy. There have been times when I've reached for him, and he's instinctively pulled away. That could be an indicator. What do you know of the family?"

"Not much, but I think it's time I found out. I can't bear the thought of the children being abused."

"That may be the reason for her issues with absenteeism last year, too, but we shouldn't assume."

"What should we do? I feel like we should report our suspicions."

"Do you feel comfortable having a conversation with their mom?"

"Not really. I have no idea how to broach the subject other than straight on, but these kids deserve better."

"Let's think about it tonight and come up with a plan. I believe we have to start with Teresa, but we can't meet in the home if there's a chance she could be in danger or too intimidated to talk freely."

"Maybe we could invite her to join us for an afternoon conference after school. You could watch the children while I talk with her. She knows my face, and it may be easier to talk to someone she's familiar with," Faith suggested.

"That's not bad, but let's think it through first." Patrice finished her coffee. "On a lighter note, how are you enjoying being a teacher again?"

"The energy and desire to learn from the kids have been refreshing. I don't understand how they could be pushed aside at the city school. They concentrate, listen attentively to my every word, and work hard to please me with their assignments. I couldn't ask for better students."

"I believe we've created a safe environment for them here, and they realize the opportunity they have been given." Patrice smiled. "I stopped for gas this morning and asked Logan if she could teach the students how to do an oil change on my car. She seemed pretty excited."

"She's loving the time spent teaching them, and she says several are talented."

"That's encouraging. I'd like to see all the students through graduation. Only one is turning sixteen soon, and I hope we can keep her in school."

"Could we propose some on-the-job training with the older kids? Maybe just a day or two a week at Miss Ruth's, with Logan at the garage or stocking at the general store?" Faith hoped for a positive answer.

"I think we have free rein to do what we need to keep these kids in school. Maybe we should visit the general store manager and Miss Ruth to discuss free help. If they are willing, I can run it past the superintendent. I know Logan and Miss Ruth are already on board."

"No doubt about Logan. She's having fun."

†

Logan woke from her long nap and showered before heading downstairs. She could hear her dad in the kitchen and walked in to find him cooking grilled cheese sandwiches and French fries. "These look good," she told him as she took a fry off the plate and popped it into her mouth. "What are you drinking tonight?"

"I'll have some tea, please. Did you get some rest?"

"Yes, I did. Thank you for sending me home. I feel much better now."

"You've got to be on your toes at all times when you're making a delivery."

"Did you ever get stopped?"

"Only once, but thankfully I had already made the drop. It took some quick thinking, but I told the officer I was returning from visiting a lady friend in the city. Thankfully, he bought the story. I think I got a few more gray hairs that night."

"That was brilliant."

"Do you have a cover story?"

"I do. I kept an old carburetor we replaced and cleaned up. I keep it in a box with an undated receipt in my truck. I plan to tell them I made a late run into town for an urgent part and decided to have dinner and see a movie since we have very few options here." Logan shrugged. "I hope I never have to use it as an excuse, but it's the best I could come up with."

"Very crafty, and the fact you're a mechanic makes it believable. Once they see you're from here from your license, they will understand the town rolls up at sundown."

Curtis placed a plate of fries between them and their sandwiches on the table.

"Thanks for cooking tonight."

"I can't let you leave on an empty stomach."

"Faith will probably try to feed me, too, but I want to talk to her about the Jerry Morgan situation and get her thoughts. I think she was planning to talk to Patrice today for advice."

"I know you're grown, but be careful around him. He can be mean as a snake."

"I will, Dad."

Logan brushed her teeth and grabbed her keys before heading to the door. "I'll try to not be too late."

"Just be careful," Curtis said.

"Thanks again for supper." Logan grinned and walked outside.

†

The moon had just risen, and a beautiful full harvest moon glowed as she drove to Faith's. Faith was sitting on the porch steps drinking coffee and playing with Finder when she arrived. "Hey, sweetie," she called out when she stepped out of the truck. "You got another cup?"

"Sure do. Come on in," Faith said. "I've just been enjoying this great night and that beautiful moon."

"It is beautiful. I could probably drive without headlights as bright as it's shining." Logan took the cup Faith offered and nodded to the table. "Can we talk for a few minutes?"

Faith sat beside her. "What's up?"

"I talked to Dad about Jerry Morgan last night, and what he told me was disturbing." Logan told her Jerry's story. "When I went to bed, I had trouble falling asleep and then had a nightmare about Sadie and couldn't get back to sleep. So, I got up, got ready for the day early, and drove to their house. I watched the house until he left at about five and then waited until a light came on in

139

the kitchen. I confronted Teresa when I looked through the window and saw the bruise around her eye. She collapsed in tears and confided to me that he was the one who caused the bruise on Sadie's arm, and he'd been whipping Chuck for perceived disrespect of him." Logan took a sip of coffee. "Teresa claims she has tried to get Jerry to seek help for his drinking, but he doesn't admit to having a problem."

"I talked with Patrice today about our suspicions, and she recommended having a conference with Teresa at the school."

"You better do it soon. Jerry will be back in two days," Logan warned.

"I will call her tomorrow and set it up for Thursday before he returns. Thanks for all the information. If something isn't done, I fear for her safety and the kids."

Logan nodded. "Teresa told me Chuck was getting frustrated with the whippings, and I don't blame him. He's getting to the age he may start physically rebelling against his father, which may escalate things quickly. He's a good kid, and I'd hate to see something bad come to him."

"I agree. As Chuck grows and gets stronger, he may feel a need to protect his mom and sister from his dad. Do you think it would be smart to get advice from Cal?"

"It can't hurt. Do you want me to give Cal a call?"

"No. Let me do it from a teacher's point of concern. If it gets ugly, I don't want to involve you in this." Faith could see the muscles of Logan's jaws clenching in anger. She reached out and covered Logan's hand with hers. "I promise you I will let you know if there's something you can help with. You are always my first call."

Logan nodded. Faith could feel the heat of her frustration radiating from her eyes and body. "Are you coming back here tonight?"

"No, I told Dad I would be late. I'll sleep in and get ready for our field trip on Friday. I am so excited to have the kids at the shop."

"No more excited than they are, I promise you. I thought Chuck would explode when we mentioned the trip."

That made Logan smile. "He's got a genuine interest and some talent with a wrench. I could easily see him attending a trade school to become a certified mechanic."

"What a great career that could be for him," Faith replied.

"I should probably get a move on," Logan said. "Moonlight's a wasting," she joked.

"I'll see you Friday night. Patrice is bringing the kids, right?"

"Yeah, but I have some beautiful steaks that I need you to cook for us."

"Sounds wonderful. See you soon. Love you."

"I love you, too."

†

The double order was a tight fit, but they managed to store it in the hidden compartment. Logan kissed Faith and hit the road. Logan planned to drive to one of the twenty-four-hour stores to buy moon pies for the station. After the oil change and tire rotation, she would treat the kids to RC colas and moon pies and still have plenty left for herself and Curtis. Logan drove as quickly as she dared to the payment pick-up spot and delivered the Holy Water after confirming the payment. When she eased back onto the highway, she drove to the city to make her purchases.

Logan left the store with much more than she had planned, wearing a smile. Bags were filled with six boxes of moon pies, a bag of tennis balls for Finder, and the unique blend of coffee Faith enjoyed. Once she cleared the city limits, she raced for home. As she neared the Morgan home, she slowed. The house was dark, and there was no sign of Jerry's truck in the yard. "Rest easy," she said as she drove past.

She had made good time even with the additional stop to shop. Logan climbed into bed at two and dreamed of being chased. Her laughter filled the truck's cab when she pulled into a cornfield and watched the cruiser fly past. She took an alternate route in her dream and made it home safely.

†

Faith brought Patrice current on the information Logan had found about the Morgan family. "Go ahead and call Teresa so we can meet with her tomorrow," Patrice suggested.

"I plan to call Cal today, too, for some advice," Faith said.

"Not a bad idea. Go make your calls before the kids get here. What's on the menu for this morning?"

"French toast and bacon."

"I can go ahead and get the bacon in the oven." Patrice smiled.

"Make sure we have soft butter, too, please."

"Consider it done."

Faith's first call was to Teresa, who reluctantly agreed to come for a conference the next day. Classes would be over, and the rest of the students would be on their way home with Toby. Her next call was to Cal, who agreed to stop by later in the afternoon.

†

Elizabeth was the oldest student and the first to come off the van. She rushed into the kitchen. "Will you teach me to make French toast?" she asked Faith.

"I'd love to," Faith answered. "Get the milk and a carton of eggs from the refrigerator, please." Faith turned to Chuck. "Will you bring us plates?"

"Paper or the good stuff?" he asked with a grin.

"I think paper will be fine."

"What can I do?" Sadie asked.

"You, my dear, can be this morning's supervisor, and the rest of you can help Ms. Patrice set up the classrooms before breakfast." Faith picked Sadie up and sat her on the counter safely away from the stove. She looked at Sadie. "Do you think you can put butter on these as Elizabeth finishes them?"

Sadie nodded with a huge smile on her face.

Patrice set up a step stool for Sadie to allow her to reach the counter. "Spread it evenly on the bread as Elizabeth puts them on plates. Got it?"

"Yes, ma'am."

"Chuck, will you put cups on the table and bring the milk and juice?"

"Yes, ma'am. The syrup, too?" he asked when he opened the refrigerator door.

"I guess that might help," Faith replied. "Better put down some napkins, too. I think we may get messy."

The timer went off, and Faith pulled out a large pan of bacon. She placed it on two plates and set it on the tables. "Please tell Ms. Patrice she can bring the kids and start pouring drinks. Elizabeth and Sadie are on a roll."

†

Cal stopped by later and was welcomed with coffee and cookies the students had made that afternoon.

"We need your advice on something from the law enforcement point of view," Faith said after she thanked him for stopping to meet them.

"I'll do my best. I'll know more once I find out the topic." Cal grinned.

"If we suspect physical abuse at home for any of our students, what should be our course of action?" Faith asked.

Cal's grin turned into a frown. "Is this happening, or are you asking in case it happens?"

Faith shot Patrice a worried look. "We have some suspicions but have not confirmed anything yet."

"One of the students came to school with a bruise on her arm, and you could see distinct fingerprints where someone grabbed her. When Faith questioned her about it, she couldn't remember what happened."

"Have you spoken to the parents?"

Faith ducked her head. "We haven't. Logan confronted the mother and told her there are options for her to get help, but we don't know what to share with her when we meet tomorrow afternoon." Faith looked at Cal. "We fear this has been going on for a while between the adults but may be affecting the children in the home."

"Children? So, there is more than one?" Cal asked.

"Yes, there are two."

"Have you seen any indications of potential mistreatment from the other child?"

Patrice shook her head. "He's an older brother and is in my class. I haven't seen anything physical, but he shies away from physical contact."

"Do you feel like they are in imminent danger at present?"

"He drives a truck and won't be back in town for another day." Faith sighed. "What do we do?"

"I think you are right to talk to the mother. She does have options and needs to get away from the toxic situation. Do you think you can encourage her to call in a report if he gets violent again?"

"We will try our best," Patrice replied.

"She will need to press charges for domestic violence. It's hard to convince some women to do that. Unfortunately, our hands are tied if they don't, and the outcome is that the abuse only worsens. Too many women will not report their abusers, especially if they are the family's sole breadwinners."

Faith could hear the frustration in Cal's voice. "If we see any additional physical evidence, should we call it in as abuse?"

"It would be investigated as potential child abuse, and the children may be removed from the home for their safety. The best action is to get the mother to report it and press charges."

"If she does press charges and he is sent away, what assistance will she be able to receive? I'm sure that will be a deciding factor for her. She doesn't work. And the options are limited here."

Cal forced a smile. "I won't lie. The options here are not as plentiful as they would be in town. They could move into a women's shelter for support and safety."

Faith shook her head. "That won't happen. This is the only home she's ever known, and she won't want to uproot the kids."

"Does she have any family left in the area?"

145

"I'm not sure, but I can find out." Faith could hear the crackle of his radio. "Thank you for stopping by today. You've been very helpful."

"I'll be on duty tomorrow afternoon if you'd like me to swing by and speak to her directly," Cal offered.

"We will keep that in mind," Patrice said as Cal stood to leave.

"I hope this works out for everyone." Cal tipped his hat and left.

Patrice slumped back in her chair. "You know these people. Will we convince Teresa to call the cops on him?"

Faith shrugged. "I honestly don't know."

"Maybe if we remind her of the danger for the family. Or the risk of the kids being removed from the home. Would that be enough?"

"I think that is something we may need to make clear for her. If we see evidence, we must report it and let the professionals sort it out. It would fare much better for everyone if she reported any violence."

"Let's pray that we can convince her to do what's right tomorrow," Patrice said.

CHAPTER TEN

Faith warmed up some leftovers for dinner and sat on the porch with Finder until the sun set. She thought about the conversation they would have with Teresa tomorrow and asked her grandfather for some guidance. Once more, the eerie sound of the dormant bell rang from the church's steeple. "I know you hear me. Please show me what to do."

The air was filled with silence except for the crickets chirping. Not even a breeze stirred the night. Faith sighed deeply, and Finder placed her head in her lap. Faith's hand stroked the dog's body. "I wish you could talk sometimes," she told Finder. "I'm sure you could advise me what to do."

Finder whined and looked at Faith with soft, whiskey-colored eyes.

"You're such a good girl. Let's get ready for bed."

†

Logan fell asleep thinking about Faith. She couldn't wait to have the kids in the shop for their field trip. Patrice would drop her car off on her way to the church, and Logan would give her a ride. When she slipped into a dream state, Logan watched as an older Sadie watched Chuck graduate from high school. They both looked so happy. Logan's eyes searched the crowd at the gathering, and she felt her breath catch as Faith was sitting on the stage, even more beautiful than she was now. Faith turned to lock eyes with her in the dream, and Logan's heart pounded in her chest.

†

Faith tossed and turned for hours until her exhausted body finally succumbed to deep sleep. She was surprised to dream about young Sadie. It appeared to be a few years later, and they were at the graduation of her brother Chuck. They both shared radiant smiles, and Chuck lifted his diploma above his head. Faith's eyes searched the crowd and found Logan sitting next to Teresa. Logan's hair had a few gray streaks, but she was even more handsome. Teresa wore the smile of a proud mother. Logan smiled when Logan's eyes met hers, and Faith felt her heart melt. Logan made the sign for love and rubbed her hand above her heart. "I will love you forever, too," Faith mumbled.

The dream was fresh in her mind when she woke up the next morning. "Was that your answer, Grandfather?" Faith was more confident about her talk with Teresa and started the coffee pot while she showered.

†

Logan was arranging the moon pies on a small rack she found in the garage when she heard Patrice pull up. "Good morning," she said.

"Where do you want me to park her?" Patrice asked.

"You can pull in front of the large bay. Let me grab my keys, and I'll drive you to school."

Patrice nodded and parked the car.

Logan opened the door for her to climb into Lightning and then walked around the truck. When she climbed inside and cranked the engine, her hand flew to the volume control on the radio. She looked at Patrice. "Sorry. I like it loud."

Patrice smiled back. "I can tell."

"I've got AC, but it won't cool down between here and the church. Are you okay with the windows down?"

"I love the fresh air."

Logan waved to her dad and drove to the church.

Logan pulled to the side entrance. "I'll see you around nine, right?"

"Yes, you will. As soon as we finish up morning lessons."

"I've got snacks for the kids after we finish your work." Logan grinned.

"I look forward to watching the students. Thank you again."

"I am, too."

Patrice stepped out of the truck.

"Tell Faith I'll be out at five tonight."

"Sure will. Thanks for the ride."

†

149

Logan paced the garage until she saw the van from the school arrive. "Finally," Curtis said. "I won't have to mop that section of floor for a month?"

Logan shot him a grin before walking out to greet her students. The two boys and one of the girls from Patrice's class piled out of the van. "Good morning, guys."

"Morning, Logan," Chuck said.

Patrice walked around. "Several girls decided to stay back and help Faith with lunch."

"No problem. This is a perfect size for today's class." She looked at Patrice. "Will you drive your car into the bay? I'll give you directions."

"Sure," Patrice said. "Would you mind if I get some photographs, too?"

Logan looked at her students. "Okay, with y'all?"

"Let her rip," Elizabeth said.

Logan guided Patrice to pull her car onto the hydraulic lift and opened her door. "You can watch over there, and you won't be in our way." She pointed to a spot beside Curtis.

She moved over to a remote unit. She explained how to lift the vehicle to provide access to the oil pan. She handed the remote to Elizabeth. "Will you do the honors? Go until I signal you to stop."

Elizabeth pressed the button until Logan signaled her. "That part was easy. Chuck, will you roll the stand with the oil reservoir lift pan to us?"

Logan turned to the other young man. "Mike, are you strong enough to remove the plug?" She handed him a tool.

"Yes, ma'am," he answered excitedly.

"Chuck, you need to pump that lever with your foot to lift the reservoir once we get it in place."

"What happens with the dirty oil?" Mike asked.

"It gets picked up and recycled into other products. Other types of petroleum products and heating oil are primary uses."

"I didn't know that," Patrice told Curtis.

"Mike, can you identify the oil pan plug?"

"Right here." He pointed to the plug.

Logan nodded. "That's right. Chuck, lift the pan a few inches so we don't get an oil bath, please."

"Yes, ma'am," Chuck said and positioned the lift.

"When you pull the plug, gravity will rush the oil quickly, so you must move fast. But don't lose the plug. Got it?"

Mike nodded. Logan watched him place the wrench on the plug. "Righty tighty, lefty loosey." She heard him whisper.

He began turning the wrench until the plug popped into his hand. Mike's eyes flew open with surprise, but he didn't drop the part.

"Okay, we'll let that drain for a few minutes. Chuck, do you know what this is?" She held up another tool.

Chucked beamed. "That's an oil filter tool."

"Very good. Would you pull the filter for us?"

"Sure," Chuck answered and placed the loop around the oil filter and tightened it to fit securely.

When the filter was loose, she instructed Chuck to drain the oil in the pan and then toss the used filter.

The flow of oil had slowed to a steady drip. "Chuck, will you lower the pan a foot, please?" She looked at the eager students. "Can someone tell me why it's important to rotate tires?"

"To keep them wearing evenly," Mike stated.

"That's correct. How often?"

Mike answered, "Dad says every two oil changes or every seven to eight thousand miles."

"Very good," Logan answered. "We will remove and rotate Ms. Long's tires while we wait for all the oil to drain. Who wants to go first?"

"I do," Elizabeth answered first.

Logan demonstrated how to use the impact wrench to remove the lug nuts after she removed the hub cap. "Put some pressure on it so it doesn't jar your teeth out," Logan teased. She stood close to Elizabeth to assist as needed.

Patrice took several shots as Elizabeth removed the first lug nut.

"Wow, that's powerful," Elizabeth stated.

"Much easier than if you have to do it manually, like if you have to change a flat."

"Will we learn that, too?" Elizabeth asked.

"Yes, ma'am, you will in another lesson."

"Mama always seems to get a flat tire, and it takes forever for Daddy to come or us to flag someone down for help," Elizabeth said.

"You will be able to change it for her," Logan said. "Mike, will you help Elizabeth remove the tire? It is much heavier when it's up in the air."

Mike and Elizabeth pulled the tire off and rolled it toward the front of the car. "Who's next?"

After all four tires were rotated, Logan instructed Mike and Chuck to replace the plug and add a new oil filter. She checked both for tightness, so there wouldn't be a leak. Everyone stepped from under the car. "Ms. Lift Operator, will you bring the car back down?" she asked Elizabeth.

"Pop the hood for us, Chuck."

"You know, back in my day, we had you use a can opener and funnel to replace the oil," Curtis told them. "These twist tops make it much easier. You still need to be careful not to spill oil on the engine parts."

Logan taught the kids how to check the oil and add the correct amount of new oil. "Lady and gentlemen, you have completed your first oil change and tire rotation."

Logan, Curtis, and Patrice clapped for them. "May I get a picture of the four of you together?"

"Sure," Logan said and stood next to Mike.

Patrice snapped several shots.

"Did anyone work up an appetite?" Logan asked.

"We can always eat, Logan," Chuck said.

"Wash up and meet me in the office. Dad, do you want to do the honors?"

"Yes." He grinned at Logan.

When the kids returned from washing their hands, Curtis handed each of them an RC cola. "What's an RC without a moon pie?"

"Naked," Chuck answered.

"I couldn't have answered that better if I tried," Curtis told him. "Chocolate or banana?"

After they finished the snack, Patrice turned to Logan. "I'll get Toby to drop me by when he takes the kids home," Patrice said. "You did a wonderful job with the class."

"Thanks. It was fun. Free labor, too." Logan winked.

†

Faith took a deep breath as she sat across the table from Teresa and released it slowly. "I won't waste your time beating around the bush. I know you've talked with Logan."

Teresa nodded. "She came by the other morning."

"We want you to know if Jerry is being abusive to you and the kids, you have support and options. Sadie came to school with a suspicious bruise on her arm, and she wouldn't say how she got it."

Teresa pulled a tissue from her pocket. "Jerry grabbed her by the arm too roughly."

"Have you ever tried to talk him into getting help with his drinking and anger issues?"

"He won't admit he has a problem. I've tried pleading with him to get help, which usually turns out poorly for me."

Faith reached out and covered Teresa's hand. "I talked to a friend in law enforcement."

Teresa's eyes grew wide with fear.

"No names were mentioned, but Patrice and I had to know what we should do. Teachers are mandatory reporters if they suspect abuse or neglect in the home. The last thing we want to happen is for Chuck and Sadie to be removed from the home by social services, but that's better than one or both of them getting hurt." Faith looked Teresa in the eyes. "You're an adult, and they are defenseless children. It's your responsibility to protect your babies."

"The last thing I want is for either of them to feel his wrath when he's drinking, but he's the only one that brings any money into the home."

"There are other options for support. Do you have any family in the area you can lean on?"

"My mom is still alive, but she struggles with social security to live on. I can't lay this burden on her."

"You used to work at Miss Ruth's part-time, didn't you?"

"Yeah, until I missed more work than I was doing because I couldn't hide the bruises."

"I bet she'd hire you back," Faith suggested. "I've got to ask you something critical to moving forward. Will you call the cops next time he starts punching you? Most importantly, will you press charges for domestic violence against Jerry?"

Teresa broke into tears and buried her face in her hands.

"Teresa, let me be blunt. If he hurts one of the kids, you can be charged for child endangerment, and you will lose the kids." Faith sighed. "There are women's shelters in the city that will take you in and protect you whenever you're ready. They will help with support and help you get on your feet."

Teresa shook her head. "The house is the only home the kids have ever known, and they love to come to school here."

"Then it's up to you to take action. I worry for Chuck. As he gets older and bigger, he may try to protect you and get seriously hurt, or he could make a mistake he'd pay for with the rest of his life."

Teresa nodded. "I see him get so angry at his father. It's like he's waiting until he's strong enough to take him on."

"Is there a gun in the house?"

"Not that I know of," Teresa replied.

"You will have the community's support to do what's right by those kids. We always pull together."

"I am tired of being scared whenever I hear his truck pull up."

"Will you call the cops then? Get that ball rolling?"

Teresa nodded. "If I can."

"If you can't, teach Chuck how to do it. He's old enough to have that responsibility."

"He's begged me to call, but I've been too scared." Teresa glanced up at the clock. "It's getting late, and he's supposed to come home tonight. I need to get supper started. That makes him mad if he comes home and supper isn't ready."

Faith nodded. "I want you to understand this. I will call if I see any evidence that he is abusing either of your kids. No second chances to talk to you. I will report what needs to be done."

Teresa nodded and stood. "I understand. Thank you for trying to help."

"It's all on your shoulders now, Teresa. You can call and talk to either of us at any time."

"Thanks." Teresa rushed out of the school, gathered her kids, and left.

†

Patrice walked in with Finder on her heels. "How'd it go? She left here like her hair was on fire."

"As good as it could, I guess. I laid everything out for Teresa. She had to rush home to get supper started. The ball is in her court. I pray she does the right thing."

"You've done everything you can at this point."

Finder whined with a ball in her mouth.

"We were playing fetch. I swear Finder can go for hours," Patrice said.

"It seems like it sometimes." Faith took the ball from Finder. "Let's lock up and call it a week."

"That sounds good to me. Remind me to show you the pictures I took this morning. The kids had a great time with Logan."

"I bet Logan had a blast, too. She's been waiting for this day all week."

Patrice picked up her purse, and they walked out to her car. "Do you have plans for the weekend?"

"Logan is coming out tonight to grill steaks. I think we may do some shopping tomorrow. Who knows?" Faith grinned. "What about you?"

"I have a date tomorrow night."

"A date? With who? When did this happen?" Faith grilled her.

"Cal asked me out for dinner and a movie."

"Oh, Patrice. That's fantastic. Cal is a good man."

"I think so, too," Patrice said with a blush. "See ya Monday."

"Yes, ma'am, you will."

Faith turned and hurled the ball for Finder.

†

Faith had just finished tossing a salad and wrapping corn and potatoes for the grill when she heard Logan pull into the drive. Finder bolted for the door, and Faith removed two bottles of beer from the fridge.

"Welcome home," she said and handed Logan a beer.

"Thanks. I need that," Logan said.

They sat together on the porch, and Logan tossed the ball for Finder. "I had so much fun with the kids this morning. They did really well, too."

"Patrice said they didn't stop talking about the experience all day. We got busy, so she didn't show me the pictures she took."

Logan frowned. "You met with Teresa today, didn't you? How'd it go?"

Faith shrugged. "As good as I could hope for, I guess. I'm not convinced Teresa will press charges."

Logan reached over and stroked Faith's cheek. "You did the best you could by talking to her. She has to be the one to make

157

the decisions moving forward. Hopefully, she will do what's right for those kids."

"Only time will tell. I did warn Teresa that I would report potential abuse if I see any evidence on either of the kids."

"Well, not only are you a caring person to do the right thing, but as a teacher, aren't you a mandatory reporter?"

"Yes. I hope I made that clear."

"I've no doubt you did, my love. When you are passionate about something, you get persuasive."

"I don't know if that's a compliment or an insult?" Faith feigned with a pout.

"Most definitely a compliment."

Logan tossed the ball. "I'm going to light the grill and shower if that's okay with you."

"That's fine. I've got everything ready for you." Faith accepted Logan's hand. "I might fry up a few slices of bacon for our potatoes. Would you like some sautéed onions for the steaks?"

"I wouldn't turn either one of them down. Maybe we can watch the start of the playoffs tonight? I'd love for the Braves to win."

Faith nodded. "That's good for me." She walked inside while Logan lit the grill.

Logan dropped their empty bottles in the trash.

†

Teresa and the kids were later than expected getting home, and of all times for Jerry to arrive home early, this wasn't a good night. "Oh dear," Teresa said when she turned into the drive and saw his truck. "I thought we'd have some cheeseburgers and fries tonight. Does that sound good?"

"Sounds great, Mom," Chuck replied.

"Go change out of your school clothes, and I'll start dinner," she said as they left the car.

Teresa entered the house and immediately went to the kitchen to start supper. Jerry was already sitting in his recliner, drinking a beer and watching television.

"Where have you been so late?" Jerry growled from the living room.

"I had a teacher conference today at the school. I'm sorry it ran later than I thought. I didn't expect you home this early. I'll have supper ready shortly."

"Good. I'm hungry. Bring me another beer before you start cooking."

Teresa removed a beer from the fridge and carried it to him. Jerry grabbed her wrist. "I don't care where you were, but on the days I come home, I expect you to be here with supper on the stove. Got it?"

"Yes, I'm sorry. I wasn't thinking."

Jerry took the new beer and handed her the empty bottle. "You never think."

Teresa rushed back to the kitchen and started making hamburger patties as the bacon cooked in the pan.

She heard Chuck enter the living room and try to engage his dad in a conversation. "Guess what I did at school today?"

"What did you do? You flew through here so fast I thought maybe you'd shit your pants."

"Naw, I just wanted to change outta my school clothes. I changed the oil and rotated tires on a car today."

"You did that at school?"

"No, sir, we went to Bronson's garage, and Logan taught us how."

"Hmmmftt. I reckon she'd know how. She's nothing more than a diesel dyke."

Chuck didn't understand his dad's comment. "Maybe next time you work on your truck, I could help you."

Jerry glared at Chuck. "You change the oil on a car, and now you think you're a mechanic? Don't let them fill your head with dreams, kid. They all turn into nightmares." He looked around Chuck. "Why don't you go help your ma and let me watch the news?"

"Yes, sir." Chuck hung his head in disappointment. He had thought his dad would be pleased.

Teresa took him in her arms for a hug. "I am very proud of you," she whispered.

"What can I help with, Ma?"

"You can bring me the lettuce, onion, and tomato from the fridge. Then you can set the table."

†

Jerry had finished off a twelve-pack by the time they finished supper. Teresa silently prayed he'd watch the ball game and drink until he passed out.

"That was a great supper, Ma," Chuck said.

"Thank you. Will you help your sister get started on her bath while I clean up here?" Teresa asked.

"Sure. Come on, Sadie," Chuck called to his sister.

Teresa could see Jerry's eyes begin to glaze over from the alcohol. She knew she would need to tread carefully tonight. "Did you get enough to eat?"

"Yes. Those were some good burgers." Jerry almost smiled.

Teresa could remember when they were younger and how his smile could light up a room. She hadn't seen that part of Jerry for a long time. She stood and started clearing the table.

"Bring me another beer. I'm going to watch the ball game, so make sure the kids stay quiet," he warned.

Teresa nodded and brought him a beer.

Jerry moved into the living room and waited for the game to start.

Teresa tried to be as quiet as possible as she cleaned the kitchen. Chuck returned to the kitchen and announced Sadie was in the tub. Teresa put a finger to her lips to warn him to be quiet. "Will you take the garbage to the road and check the mail?"

Chuck nodded and removed the bag from the kitchen. Tomorrow was their weekly trash pickup, so he took the can to the road and opened the mailbox. It contained letters he presumed were bills and the weekly sale flyer. He carried the mail into the house and forgot about being quiet. The screen door slammed loudly behind him.

"Dammit, Chuck. What did I tell you about not slamming the door?" Jerry shouted from his recliner.

"I'm sorry, Dad. I wasn't thinking."

"There seems to be a lot of that going on around here tonight. I don't know why we bother sending you to school if you can't remember something as simple as that. Bring me a beer and the mail. Probably nothing more than fucking bills. Toss that flyer in the trash. We can't afford anything they claim is on sale anyhow."

Chuck handed him the mail and took his empty bottle. He dropped the flyer in the trash and took his dad a new beer.

"Now get lost. The ball game is about to start. Unless you want to man up and watch it with me."

"I'd like that." Chuck walked into the kitchen and poured a glass of tea. He looked at his mom and shrugged.

"Check on your sister first, please." Teresa was putting away the clean dishes.

When Chuck reached her room, Sadie had finished bathing, dressed, and was in bed. "Are you okay?"

"Yes. Be careful, Chuck. He has that crazy look in his eyes tonight."

Chuck nodded. "Hopefully, he will fall asleep soon."

"I hope so, too," Sadie said and pulled the covers up to her chin. "I love you, Chuck."

"I love you, too, Sades," he teased her with a nickname. "Cartoons in the morning." He winked and left the room.

"Take these to your ma," Jerry said and handed Chuck the bills.

"Are you okay?" he asked Teresa. "Sadie is in bed. Said she was sleepy," he lied.

"Good," Teresa answered. "A hot bath will make you sleepy."

†

Jerry seemed in a good mood until the Braves allowed the other team to tie up the game. Teresa and Chuck flinched every time he shouted obscenities at the television. Teresa could feel the anger rising in him.

"Chuck, why don't you head off to bed?" she suggested.

"Stay the fuck where you are. You can watch another inning or two, can't you, boy?"

"Yes, Dad."

He turned an icy glare at Teresa. "Why don't you go make some brownies? My sweet tooth is acting out."

Teresa turned on the stove to preheat while she mixed the batter.

"Come on, you fuckers. Hit the damn ball," Jerry screamed and tossed an empty bottle at the television. Luckily, he was too drunk to aim. "Pick that up and get me another, Chuck."

When the game ended, the Braves had pulled off a win. "That was too close for comfort. I had ten bucks riding on that game." He growled and stomped into the kitchen. "Are those damn brownies ready yet?"

"They need to cool for a few minutes. They are too hot to eat. Do you want some milk to go with them?"

"Fucking yes, I do. Get some for Chuck, too."

Teresa filled two glasses of milk and cut two large brownies for them. She worried they were still too hot to eat. "Be careful. They are still warm."

Chuck used caution and waited for his dad to take a bite.

"What is this shit? Don't you know by now that I don't like nuts in my brownies?" Jerry spat the brownie on the table. "Get rid of this shit."

Chuck took a bite. "I'll eat them, Ma. They taste good."

Jerry swung at Chuck and knocked the brownie from his hand. "Not in my fucking house, you won't."

Chuck's first instinct was to bow up to his dad, which was a huge mistake.

"Do you think you're finally man enough to take on your old man, little boy?" Jerry called him out and let out an evil-sounding laugh. "Come on then, give me your best shot." Jerry kicked the chair away as he stood.

Chuck's hands clenched into fists.

"Chuck, don't please," Teresa said.

"Chuck, don't please," Jerry mocked her. "Come on, Mama's boy. Let's see what you've got."

Chuck swung at his much taller dad and barely made contact before Jerry wrenched his arm behind his back. "What kind of pussy swing was that?" He pushed Chuck away. "Let me show you how it's done." He punched Chuck in the face and knocked him across the room.

Chuck stumbled to his feet and charged toward his dad when Teresa stepped between them. "Stop it," she screamed at Jerry. "He's your son, for God's sake."

"At least that's what you tell me. The little shit needs a reminder of who's boss." Jerry swung again, striking Teresa, and blood sprayed across the room.

"No, Chuck," Teresa begged as she wiped the blood from her cheek. "Just go to your room."

"You ain't getting off that easy, boy." He grabbed Chuck, threw him against the wall, and pinned him there with a forearm across his throat.

Chuck was gasping for breath, and his face was turning red. Jerry was drawn back to strike him when Teresa sprang into action. She grabbed the first thing she could, a frying pan, and struck Jerry in the head. She could hear the sickening crunch of bone when the pan made an impact, and Jerry slithered to the floor with blood gushing from his head. Teresa dropped the pan and covered her face with her hands.

"You're okay, Mama," Chuck said. "I'm so sorry."

Teresa removed her hands. "Go get your sister. We need to get out of here."

Chuck raced down the hall and grabbed Sadie out of bed. He put a robe around her and helped her put her shoes on. He picked her up and rushed back down the hall.

Teresa bent over Jerry and couldn't tell whether he was still breathing. When she heard Chuck return, she pointed to the door. "Get in the car, and I'll be right there."

Chuck raced past to prevent Sadie from seeing the pool of blood around their dad.

Teresa gagged at the coppery smell of the pooling blood, and when a drop fell from her face, she realized she, too, was bleeding. She grabbed a hand towel and rushed to the door with her pocketbook in hand.

†

When Teresa arrived at the car, Chuck had Sadie belted into her booster seat. She climbed into the driver's side and wiped the blood from her face. "Chuck, get the keys from my purse, please."

Chuck quickly located the car keys and handed them to his mother. Her hand was shaking so intensely she couldn't get the key in the ignition, so Chuck took the keys from her and started the car.

"Where are we going?" he asked.

"I don't know, but away from here right now. I need to think." Teresa threw the car in gear and headed into town. She knew there was no place to seek refuge in the town, so she headed to a small park where she took the kids to play. The park was pitch black when she arrived and parked out of sight under a large tree. Teresa felt hot and rolled the windows down to let a cool breeze inside the car.

"Are you okay?" Chuck asked. "You're still bleeding."

He took the hand towel from her grip and blotted at her busted lip. "I'm sorry I angered him. I should have known better."

"It wasn't you, baby." She reached and softly stroked Chuck's cheek. "He was looking for a fight. We've been eating brownies with walnuts for years."

"I just don't know why he has to be so mean to us."

Teresa sighed. "It's the drinking. I wish I could get him to stop. He used to be so different."

"What can I do, Mama?"

"Watch over Sadie, and just let me think." Teresa laid her head back against the headrest.

Chuck looked into the back seat and was glad Sadie had fallen asleep. He reached over to hold his mother's hand and prayed the bastard was dead.

†

Jerry's eyes were fuzzy when he woke. He tried to sit up, and his hands slipped in the congealing blood on the floor. "What the fuck?" he groaned and lifted his hand to his throbbing head. "The bitch hit me with a frying pan," he yelled to the empty kitchen. "She will pay dearly for that."

Jerry managed to rise to his feet and searched the house for his wife and children. When he realized they were gone, he howled with rage and rushed toward the kitchen. Jerry looked out the window and saw Teresa's car was gone. He jerked the refrigerator door open and took out his last beer. Jerry angrily twisted off the top, tossed it across the room, and stormed to the door. He would find them by God and drag her back home. She was not taking his kids away from him.

†

"Damn, that was too close for comfort," Logan said when the Braves made the last out. "They had me worried for a hot minute."

"I knew they'd pull it off. Do you want a slice of pie?"

"I'd love one." Logan kissed her softly and turned off the television.

Faith was cutting into the pie when she was startled. Finder rushed past her to the door, growling, the hackles up on her spine. Faith looked at Logan, who shrugged her shoulders.

Logan walked to the front door just as a truck pulled into the yard, blaring its horn. "What the hell?" Logan ripped the door open, and Finder flew out ahead of her.

"Wait," Faith called out to them. She rushed to her desk, opened a drawer, and pulled out a small handgun.

A man stumbled out of the truck, and Logan immediately knew he was Jerry Morgan. Finder lunged forward, and he kicked at her, nearly falling to the ground. He was obviously drunk and covered in blood.

"Who are you, and what the hell do you want?" She grabbed Finder's collar until Faith arrived.

"I'm Jerry Morgan, and I'm here for my wife and kids," he slurred.

"There's no one here but the two of us," Logan stated as she stepped nearer.

"You're a fucking liar," he said and swung at Logan.

Logan caught his arm and pinned him against the truck. "You are drunk and have no business being here."

"I want that bitch of a wife and my kids. I know she was here earlier today."

"Yes, she was, but they are not here now," Logan growled back at him. "Did you hurt Teresa or one of the kids?"

"What fucking business is it of yours if I did?"

"Because if you've hurt any of them, you will answer to me. You shouldn't take your failures as a man out on your family. It's obvious you have a drinking problem and need to do something about it."

"The only drinking problem I have is I'm out of beer," Jerry said and cackled. "I will find her, and when I do, I will teach her and her mama's boy a lesson for sure."

Logan tightened her grip on Jerry. "I swear if you harm one hair on that boy, I will break every bone in your miserable body. Look at what you've become. You were a star athlete and a good person until you let the bottle get the best of you. Do something before it's too late."

Jerry tried to squirm away, but Logan held him firmly. "You need to go home, sleep it off, and do what a man would do to protect his family."

"What do you know about family, you stinking dyke?" He looked over at Faith. "Your grandfather is probably rolling in his grave because of the two of you."

"Grandfather was always supportive of Logan and me," Faith told him with a snarl. "He wouldn't condone your behavior for one damn second, though. You should be ashamed. The devil has you firmly in his grasp."

"Don't preach to me, you lezzy. You have no idea what it's like to be a husband and father."

"It's apparent you don't either," Faith shot back at him. "Do I need to call the cops?" she asked Logan.

"You don't need to do that. I'll find my way home." Jerry sneered at Faith.

"Is he safe to drive?" she asked Logan.

"He found his way here. There shouldn't be any traffic this late," Logan said. "I can follow him if you want."

"I'm a big boy, and I'll make it home just fine."

"Please get help before it's too late," Logan implored. She stepped back, releasing him from her grasp.

Jerry looked at Logan and started to step toward her until Faith raised the gun in her hand. "Get your sorry ass in the truck and leave."

Jerry's eyes grew wide when he saw the gun pointed at him. "Fine, but this ain't over yet if I find out you had anything to do with Teresa leaving tonight." He spat on the ground, climbed into the truck, and sped away.

Logan turned to Faith. "I wish I knew what was going on."

"Me, too, but it appears Teresa finally had the nerve to at least fight back. I hope she doesn't look as bad as he does."

†

They were both filled with adrenalin and too wired to sleep, so they ate their pie and settled back onto the couch to watch a movie. Logan could feel Faith relaxing in her arms when Finder stood up and went to the door. "What now? Do you need to potty?"

A soft knock sounded on the door. Logan looked out to find Teresa and her two kids. Logan pulled the door open and brought them inside. "What the hell happened?"

Teresa placed Sadie on the floor, and she rushed to Faith. Chuck followed her to the couch and sat down. Faith could see the swollen cyc that was quickly bruising Chuck's face.

"Can we step outside for a minute?" Teresa asked Logan.

"Would you two like some milk and a slice of pie?" Faith asked.

"That sounds great," Chuck answered.

Logan led Teresa to a chair on the porch. "What happened?"

Teresa broke down in tears. "I think I killed him," she said between sobs.

"Calm down and tell me what happened," Logan said.

Teresa told Logan about the night's events. "I struck him as hard as I could, and he wasn't moving. There was so much blood." She broke out in tears again.

"I can assure you that you didn't kill him, but I'm sure he'll have one hell of a headache. He was here thirty minutes before you showed up with the kids. I think we convinced him to go home and sleep it off."

"Jerry was here?" Teresa looked around, suddenly frightened.

"He was, but he's gone. You can relax."

Teresa nodded and wiped her tears away. "Let's get you inside and get you cleaned up. Chuck looked like he was hit, too. Is he okay?"

"Scared and bruised. Chuck tried to protect me, but his dad was much bigger and stronger. He pinned him against the wall, and Chuck couldn't breathe, and I feared Jerry would kill him."

"You did the right thing. I think it's best if you and the kids stay here tonight," Logan said as they entered the house.

"Pie, Mama," Sadie said when they walked into the kitchen.

"Apple, too, my favorite," Teresa said.

"Let's get you cleaned up, and you can have a slice, too. I think I'm ready for another," Logan teased.

"Faith, can we have a slumber party tonight?" Logan asked as she led Teresa from the kitchen.

"We sure can. Teresa and Sadie can have the guest room, and Chuck can have the couch."

"When he finishes his pie, can you get some ice on that cheek?"

"I've got a bag of frozen peas that will work just fine. I'll get that started right away."

†

Sadie could barely hold her head up after the pie, so Faith tucked her into bed, and Chuck sacked out on the couch. After icing, Faith gave him some Tylenol. Faith, Logan, and Teresa sat at the kitchen table.

"I'm proud of you for protecting you and your babies tonight by leaving, but you know that's just a first step."

"Yes, I know," Teresa said. "I need to call and report the abuse. Tonight was enough to scare me into that decision."

"Are you positive? You'll have to press charges to get him out of the house."

"I know. If that's what it takes for Jerry to get the help he needs, then so be it." She looked up at Logan. "Will you make the call for me?"

Logan looked at Faith. "Yes, I'll make the initial call, but you'll have to be the one to speak to the officers."

"I understand," Teresa said.

Logan took her cell phone and walked out on the porch.

†

Logan sat down in a rocker and dialed 911. She explained who she was and that she was assisting Teresa Morgan in making a domestic violence and child abuse claim against her husband.

171

"Did you say the last name was Morgan?" the dispatcher asked.

"Yes. Jerry Morgan. Why?"

"Can you hold for one second? What was your name again?"

"Logan Bronson." Logan waited for several long seconds before she heard a click.

"Officer Burns. Is this Logan?"

"Hey, Cal. Yes, it is. I've got terrible news. Jerry Morgan got drunk and was violent with his wife and son. They came out to Faith's for help."

"So, you're all out at Faith's?"

"Yes," Logan answered. "Is something else wrong?"

Cal hesitated. "Please don't say anything to Teresa, but her husband died in a traffic accident just a little while ago. He drifted into an oncoming lane and hit a logging truck head-on. He was messed up pretty badly, and it was apparent he was intoxicated."

"Fuck," Logan cried out. "Jerry was here earlier tonight looking for them, and I made him leave. I thought he was okay to make it home."

"If he had gone home, he probably would have, but Jerry was well beyond his house when he crashed. Sit tight, and I will be out as soon as I can to get the statements from everyone. Is everyone okay?"

"A bit bruised and battered, but nothing beyond first aid."

"Okay, I'll see you soon."

CHAPTER ELEVEN

Logan walked back into the house and looked at Faith. "We should probably get Chuck in your bed. Cal is on his way out, and there may be things discussed he shouldn't overhear."

"The first room on the left," Faith told Teresa.

"Let's take Finder outside," Logan stated.

"What's up? I know that look of worry on your face," Faith said when they stepped onto the porch.

"Jerry died in a crash with a logging truck. When I made the call and told them Teresa's last name, she asked if the husband was Jerry and patched Cal into the call. He was at the scene. He said not to mention anything to Teresa yet."

"Oh my God," Faith said and covered her mouth. "I was sure he could make it the short distance home."

"He could have, but he kept on driving. He was probably looking to buy more beer," Logan told her and pulled her into a hug. "We didn't do anything wrong."

"Does Cal know about Teresa hitting him with the frying pan?"

"No, I didn't mention it to him. I told him Teresa brought the kids out here for refuge. I wasn't sure if the call was being recorded."

"That was a smart thing to do. Oh my. This has turned into quite a night."

"One that is far from over," Logan said and opened the door for Finder. She leaned in and kissed Faith. "I love you. Remind me to tell you about the dream I had last night about Teresa and the kids."

"Oh, my goodness. I had one about them, too," Faith said and walked into the house. "I think I'll put some coffee on."

†

Teresa got Chuck into bed and joined them around the table. Faith poured them a cup when the coffee finished and left a cup out for Cal. He would probably need one when he arrived. He was supposed to be off duty an hour ago. Faith was thankful Cal was the officer coming out to investigate. At least she and Logan knew him, which might put Teresa at ease.

A few minutes later, Logan saw the flash of headlights through the kitchen window and walked to the door to let Cal inside.

†

"Hey, Logan," he said with a forced smile. Cal turned to the kitchen table and saw Faith with a woman who looked terrified. He saw the busted lip and the facial swelling and

174

grimaced. How could a man do that to the woman he loved? Cal was amazed by the cruelty family could enact upon one another, especially when drugs or alcohol were involved. He nodded to Faith and looked at Teresa.

"I'm Cal Burns," he said as he took a seat and opened up his notepad.

"Would you like some coffee, Cal?" Faith asked.

"That would be great."

"Mrs. Morgan, I will need to ask you several questions. Do you mind if Logan and Faith are present?"

"No, they have been wonderful to me and the kids," Teresa answered.

"Where are the children?"

"We put them to bed. They were both exhausted," Faith said as she handed him the coffee.

Cal looked back at Teresa. "I know this may be painful, but can you tell me what happened tonight?"

"My husband, Jerry, came home earlier than expected tonight from his job." She looked at Faith. "He was already home when I returned from our meeting. Jerry had begun drinking and was sitting in the living room watching television when we entered. I sent the kids to their rooms to change out of their school clothes while I started supper."

Cal took notes while Teresa told the story. He gave her a moment to pause while he sipped his coffee. "What happened next?"

"We finished dinner with only a few ugly comments to me and Chuck, our son. Chuck was excited to tell his dad about his morning with Logan at the garage, but Jerry just blew him off. Jerry kept drinking and had Chuck watch the Braves game with him while I cleaned up from dinner. Sadie had taken her bath and was already in bed."

Teresa paused for a breath.

Cal waited patiently for her to continue.

Teresa shared with him the verbal and physical abuse she and Chuck had suffered at Jerry's hands. She paused again. "When he had Chuck against the wall choking him, I knew I had to take action, so I grabbed the first thing I could reach, a skillet out of the dish drainer, and hit him in the head. Only then could Chuck break free. I told Chuck to get his sister. I had decided we had to leave or be more seriously injured. He was in such a rage," Teresa said as the tears started to flow.

Faith handed her a box of tissues.

"When you and the kids left the house, where was Jerry?"

"He was lying on the kitchen floor in a pool of blood. I tried to check him, but I couldn't tell whether he was breathing. I was so scared. I grabbed my purse and rushed out to the car."

"Where did you go?"

"I drove to the old city park downtown to think. There was nothing in town still open, so I had nowhere else to hide. Then, I remembered Faith's offer to help, and I drove the kids and me here."

Cal looked at Logan. "You said Jerry had come out here, right?"

"Yes. Jerry showed up blaring his horn, belligerent and obviously drunk. He tried to kick Finder and punch me several times until I restrained him against his truck. Jerry insisted Teresa and the kids were here; it took a few minutes to convince him otherwise. He finally calmed enough to let him go, and I encouraged him to go home and sleep it off. I thought he was sobered enough by then to make it home safely and offered to follow him home. He stated he didn't need or want that and left as quickly as he had arrived."

"Then what happened?"

"Faith and I were relaxing, watching a movie when Teresa and the kids showed up. She told us what happened, and we provided first aid to her and Chuck. Teresa asked if I would call in the report, so I did. That's when I talked to you."

"Faith, do you have anything to add?"

"No, Cal, I think they've explained it well."

Teresa looked at Cal with tears in her eyes. "What do I need to do next? I know I have to press charges against him, right? I just want Jerry to get some help. He's really not a bad man."

Cal took a deep breath. "When Jerry left here, he didn't go home. Based on his location, we can only assume he was going for more beer. I'm sorry, but he veered into the oncoming lane and was killed in an accident."

"Oh, dear God. What have I done?" Teresa said and broke into tears again.

Cal placed a comforting hand on her arm. "None of this was your fault. You did exactly what you needed to do to protect your children and yourself. If you had stayed at home, it could have been you or Chuck that was killed."

"What do I do now?" Teresa implored.

"We will help you figure that out," Faith assured her.

Cal stood to leave. "If Logan will come outside with me, I will give her some information you will need tomorrow. Right now, you need to sleep and prepare yourself to share the news with your children. Here is my card if you have any other questions. Call me any time."

Cal looked at Faith. "Can you handle things here for a while? I need Logan to go with me for a short time?"

"Yes, of course."

"I'll be back as soon as I can. Try to get Teresa to rest with one of the kids." Logan smiled at them. "Everything will be okay." Logan followed Cal to his cruiser.

†

"Thanks for coming with me. I need to document the crime scene to close out the report. Will you direct me to the house?"

"Sure." Logan gave him directions to the Morgan home. The front door was unlocked, so they walked inside. The coppery smell of blood and beer filled the kitchen. Logan knew the scent of baked brownies should have filled the kitchen, but it was hidden from her senses. Cal entered and began taking pictures with his camera. There was a large pool of congealed blood with numerous smear marks and trails of blood drips around the kitchen. The frying pan was on the floor and surrounded by blood.

"Sweet Jesus," Cal said. "I know some of this is not his blood."

"Teresa had been bleeding badly when she arrived. A hand towel was filled with blood stains from her mouth."

"The boy?"

"No blood, but he'll have a swollen face and shiner for days. I bet he'll have bruises on his throat if he doesn't already. He tried to protect his mama." Logan could feel her anger rising. "How can anyone do this to their family?"

"It's an illness," Cal said. "I'd bet Teresa has hidden whiskey scars for years."

"I know she has," Logan said. "She wouldn't do anything as long as it was just her. He is their only money coming into the house. But when he started hurting the kids, I think she finally saw the handwriting on the wall."

"Her leaving was probably the only thing that saved them from being seriously injured or killed." He pointed to the box of empty beer bottles. "There was also an empty pint jar of whiskey in the truck." Cal snapped several more pictures.

"Can I clean this blood off the floor?" Logan asked. "They don't need to come home to this."

"I'll open the windows if you can find a mop and bucket." Cal slipped his hands into latex gloves and began wiping the blood with paper towels.

Logan located a mop bucket and filled it with bleach and hot water. When Cal finished getting up what he could, she mopped the kitchen floor.

Cal peeled the gloves off and dropped them in the garbage. "I'm going to take this out. It already smells better in here."

Logan nodded as she mopped the floor. "I want to go over it with a floor cleaner to kill the bleach smell, if that's okay. I know you were supposed to be off duty hours ago."

"Don't worry about that. Take whatever time you need."

"Thanks." Logan was almost finished mopping for the second time when he returned.

Cal looked at her and shook his head. "There was another bag of bottles in the trash."

"What should she do now?"

"I've got the information in the cruiser for what hospital he was taken to. Teresa needs to make arrangements with a funeral home for burial or cremation. I recommend a closed casket if she opts for the burial."

"I can help her with that."

"I'd contact the trucking company and see what insurance he had. I know the company had at least a small policy on him. Hopefully, he had more. The truck will be a total loss, but I doubt Teresa will get much from them. Especially since alcohol was involved."

"Is it worth salvaging for scrap metal?"

"That's about all it's suitable for. Even the tires were blown. Most of the engine ended up in the passenger compartment. I'll give you the towing company's name, so maybe she can get a few hundred for scrap. They might take it to cover the towing costs if he didn't have current insurance."

"Will she be able to apply for benefits for the kids and widow's benefits from social security?"

"I would think so, and food stamps if they weren't already getting them."

"We won't allow them to go without," Logan promised. She dumped the mop water and replaced the bucket. "Not perfect, but it looks and smells better. Thank you for helping. I know that's not in your job description."

"It's all being a part of the community. I don't live here, but I feel like I'm a part. Maybe a distant part." Cal grinned.

"Will there be any legal action taken against Teresa or Jerry?"

"There's no need to tarnish a dead man's name. I'll close my report, and we'll let his death be the end of it."

"That's a relief. I don't want Teresa or the kids drug through the mud because of him."

"Amen. Let's get you home."

Cal dropped Logan back at Faith's with a handful of papers. She crept into the house at two in the morning, locked the door behind her, and found Faith asleep on the couch. Logan sat down in a recliner and removed her shoes and socks. She sat still for a long time, watching Faith as she slept.

Faith stirred in her sleep, and when her eyes opened, she found Logan watching her. "Why are you way over there?"

"I was enjoying watching you sleep."

"Come here, and you can watch from close up."

Logan climbed in behind her and wrapped an arm around Faith. "Tell me about your dream."

"That's incredible. It is almost exactly like my dream," Logan replied after Faith finished. "I guess it was your grandfather's way of letting us know everything will be all right."

"That's what I'm thinking, too. Let's try to get some sleep. Tomorrow is going to be hectic."

Chapter Twelve

Logan woke to the smell of coffee and cooking bacon. Sadie and Chuck sat on the floor watching cartoons with the volume down low. "Turn it up. I love Sponge Bob," she told them.

"Logan," Sadie called out when she heard Logan's voice. She jumped up and ran over to her. "I'm sorry if we woke you. We were trying to be quiet."

"You were very quiet, but my stomach started rumbling with the smell of bacon cooking."

"It does smell good, doesn't it? Mommy and Ms. Faith are making French toast and bacon for breakfast."

Logan slipped into her socks and walked to the bathroom to relieve her bladder. "Y'all have it smelling good."

"Get some coffee, and breakfast will be ready soon."

Chuck looked up at Logan, and she could see the bruises on his cheek and throat. "Did you sleep well?"

"I did, Logan," he answered. "Sorry, I took your bed."

"No problem. I slept just fine on the couch." Logan poured a cup of coffee and sat at the table.

"How'd you sleep, Teresa?"

"Like a rock, once I snuggled into Sadie. She's my little heater."

Faith placed a slice on two plates to get the kids started. Teresa picked up a knife to spread butter over them, and Sadie smiled. "I can do that, Mommy."

Teresa handed Sadie the butter knife. "When did you learn how to do that?"

"Are you kidding? Sadie is my best breakfast supervisor," Faith replied. "She adds her syrup and cuts it all on her own."

"Really?" Teresa pulled milk from the refrigerator.

"There's some orange juice, too, if they'd like some," Faith said.

"Yes, please," Chuck said.

"Sadie, would you like some?"

"No, Mommy."

Faith slid two slices on a plate and handed it to Logan. She shook her head. "Feed the kids first."

"Hush and eat it while it's hot. I'll have more when the kids are ready," Faith answered.

"Will you share your butter?" Logan asked Sadie.

Sadie giggled and pushed the butter dish to Logan. "Don't hog the syrup," she told Chuck.

"Who wants bacon?" Teresa asked.

All three hands went up, and Teresa served the bacon.

"Great job on the breakfast, ladies," Logan said.

"Eat up. We have plenty," Faith said.

†

After everyone was stuffed with breakfast, Faith and Teresa cleaned the kitchen. When they had finished, Teresa looked at Chuck. "Will you take Sadie and Finder out to play fetch for a while?"

"Yes, ma'am." He jumped off the couch and grabbed Finder's ball. "Let's go."

Teresa looked at Logan and Faith. "I don't know how to tell them their father is dead."

"You have to be gentle but honest with them," Faith suggested. "You can do it here with us if you want."

"I'd like that, and then we will head home. We have to face that, and the sooner, the better."

"Cal and I cleaned up what we could, but you may want to do it again," Logan said. "He also gave me some papers I need to review with you when you're ready."

"I'm ready now while the kids are playing."

Logan picked up the stack of papers Cal had given her. "The first is the number where Cal was taken last night. Do you have any idea if you will do a burial or cremation? If you choose a burial, Cal recommends a closed casket."

"I hate that the kids won't see him one last time, but I understand. Would it be bad if I opted for a cremation?"

"No, not at all. Many people prefer that." Faith looked at Teresa. "If you want to bury him, there will be a spot in the cemetery for him."

Teresa shook her head. "I don't believe he deserves that."

Logan moved to the next page. "There's a list of funeral homes that will help with arrangements. This is the tow company that towed the truck. I don't know if he had insurance, but if he did, contact the insurance company for instructions. At worst, the tow company will keep it for scrap to cover the towing expenses."

"I think he did," Teresa replied.

"Cal says the company he drove for carries a small insurance policy for all the employees. Hopefully, Jerry had more than the minimum coverage. He also recommends you contact social security to get started applying for benefits for you and the kids. Food stamps, too."

"We get some of those already and medical coverage for the kids."

"That's good. Maybe it will make the rest of the process easier. Will you need help?"

"I think I can do everything so far."

"Remember, you have a community backing you, so if you need anything, just ask."

Teresa nodded. "I surely appreciate that."

"If you need me to take you to the funeral home to make arrangements, let me know," Logan said.

"Who did you use for your grandfather?"

Faith looked at the list. "Parsons. They were good to work with."

"I'll call them later today. I think I'm ready to talk to the kids," Teresa said.

"I'll get them," Logan said.

†

When the kids sat around the table, Teresa took a deep breath. "I have some sad news to tell you. You know your dad was in a bad mood last night, right?"

Chuck's hand went to his throat, and he nodded.

"After he left last night, he was riding around and got in a car accident. Your dad was killed, and he won't be coming home ever again."

"No!" Chuck cried out. "I didn't mean it." Chuck fled the house.

The three women looked at each other with startled looks. Faith placed a hand on Teresa's arm and looked at Logan.

"Let me go after him," Logan said.

Teresa was crying as Logan left the table. Sadie told her, "Mommy, don't cry. He can't hurt us anymore."

"No, baby, he can't. I hope you will remember some of the good things about him, though."

"I'll try, Mommy."

†

Logan saw Chuck run behind the church, and she followed him. Chuck was sitting at a picnic table with his head down on the table. She could hear his sobs, and it tore at her heart for Chuck to think he was the cause of his dad's death. "Mind if I join you?"

Chuck lifted his head and wiped his arm across his face. He tried his best to hide his tears.

"It's okay to cry," Logan said as she sat beside him. "It's a sad thing."

Chuck sniffled. "I'm not sad. Does that make me bad?"

"Not at all," Logan replied. "He was mean to his family, and you have a right to be angry if that's what you're feeling."

"It's my fault," he said.

"How so?"

"By trying to stand up to him when I was still too little, and praying that he was dead."

186

Logan took a deep breath. "What you did, trying to protect your mom was courageous. Sadie is probably too young to realize what is going on, but I'm sure you've seen plenty of his bad moods."

"More than I can count. I still prayed that Dad was dead."

"He hurt you and your mother. It's normal to be angry and say or think things you later want to take back, but his behavior and poor choices cost him his life, not yours." Logan shifted on the bench. "I wish you knew your dad when he was younger. He was a great guy until he started drinking. I hope you will take this as a warning not to abuse alcohol or people."

"I wish I could remember good times with him. All I can remember is how Mama cried and how she struggled to keep us safe and happy."

"Maybe you will have some of those memories as you grow older. If not, that's okay, too. Just remember, your dad wasn't always a mean person." Logan stretched her legs in front of her. "Are you good at keeping secrets?"

"Yes, ma'am." He nodded.

"Night before last, I had a dream. You, Sadie, and your mama were in it. You were graduating from high school right here on these grounds. Sadie was a beautiful young woman, and your mama's smile was bright. She was so proud of you. I think that was a message from Faith's grandpa that everything was going to turn out all right."

"Really?"

"Your role is more important now that your dad is gone. You are the man of the house and will need to help your mama out all you can. She will have hard days and will need your love more than ever. Sadie, too, so be patient with her as I know you can be."

"I can do that," Chuck said.

"Can I ask you something?"

"Sure, Logan."

"When you have that diploma in your hands, what comes next? What do you want to do after high school?"

"Right now, I'd like to attend a trade school and become a mechanic like you. I hope to work with you on weekends and summer to learn some stuff. You won't have to pay me much, and I promise I'd work hard."

"Then we will make it happen. You'll get certified if you love the work as much as I think you do. If you change your mind between now and then, that's okay, too. You can be whatever you like and still be able to fix your own damn car."

"Truck. I want a truck like Lightning," he said.

"You know how I got Lightning?"

Chuck shook his head. "No, ma'am."

"I went to a junkyard, found a decent body, and bought it for almost nothing. Dad and I worked on her for three years until she was drivable. Nearly every cent I made went into that truck, and we did all the work except for the paint job. I'm still saving up for that." Logan winked.

"Would you help me build a truck?"

"Between Dad and me, you will have all the guidance you need. Maybe we can start looking for a body when you're out of school for Christmas break."

"I'd love that," Chuck said.

"I would, too. I miss not having a project vehicle."

"I'll save everything I can between now and then."

"In a couple of weeks, when everything settles down, we can talk about you working at the station on the weekends."

"I've got a bike, and I can get there as early as you need me."

Logan smiled and offered him her hand. "Deal. One last thing. If you ever need to talk to me about anything, you can. It will stay between us."

"Deal," Chuck said and shook her hand.

"I know your mama wants to go out to the house today. She may need your help, so be sure to help her however you can. Once the town learns about your dad, you'll start getting visitors and more dang casseroles than you can eat. I call dibs if Miss Ruth makes her chicken casserole. They are tasty." Logan smiled.

"I'll keep you posted."

"Are we good to head back into the house?"

"Yes, ma'am. Thank you for being my friend, Logan."

"I'll always be here for you, Chuck. Remember that."

Chuck nodded and stood up. He offered Logan his hand and pulled her off the bench.

Logan rubbed her back. "I'm getting too old to sit on that bench for long."

"You're not old. Just goofy," Chuck said.

"I got your goofy." Logan laughed. "Last one to the porch is a rotten egg."

Chuck rolled his eyes. "I take that back. You are old."

Logan barely reached the porch before him, and they laughed as they walked through the door. "Come on, rotten egg."

"You didn't beat me by much," Chuck said.

"Just don't ever challenge Finder. She can run circles around us."

"Are you okay, baby?" Teresa asked.

"Yes, Mama. I'm not a baby anymore. I'm the man of the house."

Teresa looked at Logan, who shrugged her shoulders.

"Still a slowpoke."

"Sadie, honey, can I still call you baby?"

189

"Yes, Mommy," Sadie answered sweetly.

"Okay, my baby and my man of the house. Let's go home."

"Call if you need anything," Faith said as they walked out to the car with them.

CHAPTER THIRTEEN

Weeks passed, and life was starting to feel normal again. Logan was at the station while her dad made a lunch run when she got the call she'd been waiting to receive. A friend of hers at a local junkyard had found the perfect body for Chuck's project. "Can I come to give it a look this afternoon?"

"Of course, you can. I haven't seen you in months."

"I'll see you later then. Thanks, Tommy."

When Curtis returned with lunch, Logan looked at him. "I need to take off early today."

"Sure. I didn't think you were cooking until tomorrow night," Curtis replied.

"We aren't. Tommy called and said he had the perfect body for Chuck's project truck. I'd like to go take a look, around four."

"You can go with one condition," Curtis said. "I need to go with you." He smiled.

191

"That would be awesome."

†

After the students left for the day, Patrice smiled at Faith. "Can I run an idea by you?"

"Like you have to ask. Spill it."

"Cal and I have been talking. He's off on Thanksgiving Day and has a new turkey fryer he's dying to try out. I don't know if you have big plans for the day, but how would you feel about hosting a Thanksgiving Day lunch on the grounds for our students and their families?"

"Can we include Toby, Miss Ruth, and Miss Betsy?"

"Absolutely. We need great desserts and someone to organize us," Patrice said. "Cal and I will buy and cook several turkeys. We can ask families to bring vegetables, desserts, or other goodies. The kids can come out and help with making some desserts and salads."

"Logan and I will go to the city for a couple of those honey-baked hams," Faith said.

"Can we ask Miss Ruth and Miss Betsy to come out tomorrow after school?"

"I'll call them, and Toby can pick them up on his way back to the school."

"I want to treat them to a feast like they've never known," Patrice said. "The kids have worked so hard. I think they need to be rewarded."

"I agree. After we meet, we can draft an invitation and send it home with the kids to get a headcount and see what each family can supply for the feast."

"I'll work on that tonight," Patrice said.

"Maybe we can do another for Christmas if this turns out well."

"That's the spirit."

✝

Curtis locked the door and turned to Logan. "Let's go."

They drove out to Tommy's junkyard and looked at several truck bodies. "This Chevy is the best of the bunch," Curtis said.

"That's what I thought, too," Tommy said. "She even has some working parts that wouldn't need to be replaced."

Logan ran her hand down the fender. She could imagine the possibilities. "How much?"

"Didn't you say this was for Jerry Morgan's boy?" Tommy asked.

"Yes, he's almost fourteen," Logan answered.

"He deserves something good after what his old man put him through. How about two hundred dollars?"

Logan saw her dad's eyebrow shoot up, and she couldn't believe she had heard the price correctly. "Two twenty-five if he likes it, and you'll tow it to our shop."

Logan pulled out her wallet and handed him the money. "I'll bring him out tomorrow if that's okay?"

"I'll be here," Tommy said. "If he's willing to pull some parts for me, we can barter items for his truck."

"I'm sure he'll jump at that," Curtis answered. "What do you know about the motor?"

"Low miles, but seized up when the owner forgot to add oil. With your guidance, I bet you can get it running."

"Logan's never met a motor she couldn't fix."

"Don't jinx me, Dad." Logan chuckled. "I'll bring Chuck out to take a look tomorrow."

"What's the story if he likes the truck?"

"I paid for it, and he'll work it off at the shop." Logan smiled.

"Sounds good. I'll try to keep an eye for good parts that will work."

"Thanks, Tommy."

"Thank you for caring so much. Those kids need all the love they can get."

"Yes, they do." She looked at Curtis. "Ready, Dad?"

When they got in the truck, Logan turned to her dad. "I'm going to drop you off for your truck and then stop by to talk to Chuck."

"I'll get supper started," Curtis said before climbing out of her truck.

"Why don't I pick you up at the house, and you can visit the Morgans with me, and we'll drive into the city for dinner?"

"I haven't been to the city in a while. Can we find someplace for two grease monkeys to eat?"

"I'm sure we can. I'll follow you home."

When they pulled up at the Morgan's, Chuck rushed to the door when they walked onto the porch. "Come on in," he said. "Mama's cooking dinner."

"Well, it's you we are here to see," Logan said.

"Y'all come on in, and Chuck can serve you some tea. Will you stay for supper?"

"Thanks, but I promised Dad a meal in the city. Smells good, though."

"So, what brings you two by today?"

194

"I want to borrow Chuck after school tomorrow if that's okay?" Logan looked at Chuck. "My friend Tommy at the junkyard called me, and he has a truck body I want you to see. Dad and I agree it could be a good project for you."

"Heck yeah. Can I, Ma?"

"I don't see why not. You can at least make a down payment on it."

"I've already agreed to pay for it and delivery to the shop if you like it. You can work it off on weekends and school breaks."

"I've got seventy-five dollars saved up," Chuck said.

"Keep that for now. Tommy will also allow you to pull parts for him when you need something for the truck."

"That sounds too good to pass on, Chuck," Teresa said.

"Will you write me a note, and I'll get Toby to drop me at the station?" Chuck asked Teresa.

"I'll drop him home when we get back."

Teresa nodded. "Fine with me."

"Thanks for the tea. We'd better get a move on, Dad. See you tomorrow, Chuck."

"Yes, ma'am, you will."

"Please get with Faith and let me know when you two can come for dinner one night. We have so much to thank you for."

"I will," Logan said. "Goodnight."

†

"How about a nice steak, Dad?"

"Sounds good, but I'm buying tonight."

"I won't argue with you. This has been an expensive afternoon."

"Tommy practically gave you that truck."

195

"That's why I went ahead and paid him. That's too good of a deal to pass on. It will make a perfect truck for Chuck."

"He could have easily gotten three times that amount."

"I think he understands what Chuck has been through the last month."

"Chuck is doing well. He's an impressive young man. I look forward to him working with me on weekends at the shop. I think it's time for you to take both days off on the weekend."

Logan looked at her dad. "That would be nice. I could always come in if there is a project needing me."

"I think me and Chuck can handle things. It's time for you to have a life before it's too late. You and Faith both work hard and deserve time together."

"Thanks, Dad."

†

Chuck flew off the van after school and rushed to find Logan. "Can we go now?"

"Grab us an RC and banana moon pie," Logan said as she washed her hands. "I'll see you tomorrow, Dad."

"Hello to Faith for me."

"Will do, Dad." Logan reached for the RC and moon pie. "What are you waiting on?" she teased Chuck.

"Have fun," Curtis called after them.

Logan cranked up the music when they turned on the highway. She popped the last bite of the treat in her mouth and washed it down with a long drink. She glanced over at Chuck, and she thought his face might break. He was smiling so hard.

"Are you kidding me?" Chuck cried out when he saw the truck.

Tommy had pulled the truck into his shop, rinsed the mud from the body, and placed it on the flatbed.

"You like her?" Tommy asked.

"She's perfect. Well, she will be one day."

"You've got two great teachers to help you with her. When you're ready for parts, you can work a few hours for me in exchange for what you need."

"Thank you, sir," Chuck said and offered Tommy a handshake.

"You better thank Logan. She's worked the deal for you."

"Oh, he has a dozen times already." Logan grinned.

"Just be sure to bring her out to show me when you get her running."

"Yes, sir, I will."

"Do we have a deal? I can drop her by the shop tomorrow morning."

Logan looked at Chuck. "I do believe we have a deal. I'll see you in the morning."

†

Logan turned the radio off on the drive home. Chuck talked non-stop. It made her heart swell to hear the excitement in his voice. She remembered making the same trip with her dad and how excited she had been.

"What should I name her?" Chuck asked.

"That will come to you when you start working on her. Don't rush it. When it feels right, you'll know. It can't be dammit to hell if you scrape your knuckles trying to break something loose."

Chuck broke out laughing. When he turned to her with a serious face, she smiled. "How did you come up with Lightning?"

"If I tell you, you have to keep it secret. Dad would blister my hide if he knew."

Chuck leaned toward Logan with interest. "I promise."

"The first time I drove her solo, it was at night, and there was a terrible lightning storm. I raced the storm front for miles trying to catch the lightning. We were going crazy fast, so I called her Lightning."

"That's cool."

"Don't ever drive that fast in a thunderstorm. I could have been killed chasing the lightning."

Chuck nodded, but Logan knew he'd never hold anything back the first opportunity he had to drive fast. He was enough like her in that aspect. "If I find out, I'll blister your hide." She smiled at him.

"Would you mind if I came by tomorrow after school?"

"Yes, tell your mom I'll bring you home. If it's not too busy, we can look at her and see what we need to get started."

"That would be awesome." Chuck grabbed his book bag and stepped out of the truck. "I'll see you tomorrow."

"Have a good night."

"You, too. Hey, Logan? Can I borrow your phone and show Mom the picture?"

"Sure." Logan pulled out her phone, brought up the picture, and handed it to Chuck.

"I'll be right back." Chuck flew toward the house.

Maybe I can get Faith to print a copy for him. Several minutes later, Chuck rushed back to her and gave her the phone.

"Thanks, Logan. I'll be dreaming about her tonight."

"See ya, Chuck."

Logan cranked up the music and drove to Faith's.

Logan walked into the house and pulled Faith into a hug. She kissed her. "You've got something smelling good."

"I hope you don't mind spaghetti. Patrice and I stayed after to discuss a plan."

Logan chuckled. "I would eat a peanut butter and jelly sandwich and be happy as long as I was with you."

"That is so sweet. Supper is ready if you're hungry. Do you want to shower first?"

"Not unless I'm offensive. I'm hungry and curious about this plan you two are cooking up."

"Go wash your hands, and I'll serve us a plate."

"That was delicious." Logan groaned after swallowing the last bite of garlic toast. "So, what are you ladies up to now?"

"Patrice and Cal want to make a Thanksgiving lunch for the kids, their families, and a few others on Thanksgiving Day. Cal has a new turkey fryer that needs some breaking in."

"That sounds like a great idea."

"Good. I signed us up for a couple of those honey-baked hams." Faith smiled at her. "Miss Ruth and Miss Betsy will meet with us after school tomorrow to help us plan. Patrice is working on an invitation, RSVP, and a spot for each family to add a dish to contribute. We will handle the meats, and they can bring the rest."

"It may be the best holiday meal ever for most of them. It's a wonderful idea. The kids will be on break, right?"

"Yes, but we can have some of them come out to help that day. They can also make all the decorations as a project."

"You know what would be fun for them?"

"What?"

"I could get a roll of that white butcher paper, and they could cover the tables and draw placemats and decorations. After the blessing, we could ask everyone to write one thing they are thankful for this year."

"I love it!" Faith said and clapped her hands.

"Before I forget, Teresa wants to know when we can have dinner with them? She wants to thank us for all of our help."

"When are you planning a run?"

"I could do Friday night or Saturday. I've been fired from working weekends."

"You what?"

"Dad is hiring Chuck to work with him on the weekends. He said it's time you and I have a life together."

"That's fantastic news. I know Chuck will be excited."

"Yes, he is. Will you print something out for me?"

"Of course. What do you need?"

"I'd like to give him a photo of his new truck. We went out today and sealed the deal with Tommy."

"Let me see." Faith reached for Logan's phone. "Oh, wow. I don't know what the insides look like, but the body looks good."

"I bet he doesn't sleep tonight. He's so excited."

"How did he get this?"

"I bought it for him, and he's going to work for us to pay it off. When he needs some parts, Tommy will have him pull some parts to barter. He made me an almost obscene deal."

"Did he know it was for Chuck?"

"Yeah. I think that's why Tommy gave us such a good deal. Tommy understands the hell Chuck's been through."

Faith nodded. "Tell her we'll come out Friday then. Do you want to get the mash started while I clean up?"

"Sure. Then I'll shower before the run starts."

"I'll see you soon then." Faith leaned down to kiss Logan. "I love you."

"Love you, too."

†

When Logan entered the still room, she smiled. Faith had already run a batch that was stacked beside the corn. "That will make tonight go much quicker." She prepared the mash for the run and lit the fire. If everything went well, they could be in bed by one. Two at the latest. Logan picked up two of the five-gallon buckets and carried them through the tunnel. "Either these are getting heavier, or I'm getting weaker." Her arms were trembling by the time she sat them on the floor. Time for a dolly. Logan grinned and climbed the steps.

Faith was almost finished in the kitchen. "When did you run a batch?"

"Last night. I couldn't sleep, so I cooked a batch."

"Good job. That will make tonight go much faster."

"That was my thinking, too. Would you mind if I make some lists while we're waiting on the drip to finish?"

"Not at all. I'm going to hit the shower. Join me?" Logan grinned.

"We might screw up the whole run if I did. We'll be done earlier than planned tonight."

"Be careful. I brought two buckets to the steps already. Damn, they were heavy. I think it's time to use a dolly."

"I think there's one in the shed we can use. I'll look for it tomorrow." Faith picked up her notepad. "Enjoy your shower."

Faith carried the three cases of jars from the still room. She wasn't strong enough to take the bucket, so she'd leave that for Logan. She sat and opened her notepad to start making notes.

201

She loved Logan's idea. They could roll them up and keep them at the school for the kids to reflect on each year. When Logan arrived, she made a list of the dishes they would need for the Thanksgiving feast.

Logan checked the drip and disposed of the head.

"What are some of your favorite dishes?" Faith asked.

"Macaroni salad, deviled eggs, potato salad, squash casserole, and pumpkin pie."

Faith added them to her list.

Logan smiled. "Homemade yeast rolls, dressing, cranberry sauce, apple pie. Hey, maybe we can make some ice cream."

"You're making me hungry," Faith teased.

†

Faith slipped the shirt over Logan's head and planted kisses from her neck to her collarbone. "You smell delicious," she breathed against Logan's skin. Her hands slipped beneath the waist of Logan's pants to slide them over her hips.

"You have too many clothes on." Logan chuckled. She helped Faith out of her pants and unbuttoned her shirt. "There, that's better," she said as she tossed the shirt aside.

Faith pressed Logan onto the bed and lay on top of her. They kissed deeply, both eager for a release. The last few weeks had been hectic, and they'd had very little time together.

Logan took Faith's hand, placing it between her legs. "I want you to come with me. I know we are both ready for some pleasure." Logan's fingertips teased Faith's opening as she felt Faith enter her deeply. Her mind swirled with pleasure. Two fingers slipped into Faith's entrance as they began a long, sensual kiss. Faith's moan filled the air as her hips pressed into Logan's hand, forcing her fingers deep inside.

Logan started a slow rhythm which built with encouragement from Faith's movements. Faith matched her movement as their bodies entwined. She could feel Faith's muscles begin to pulse against her fingers. When Faith broke the kiss, she groaned in pleasure. "Come with me, Logan."

Her request was all Logan needed to release the tide of pleasure that had built inside her. She felt her orgasm race through her body as Faith's fingers remained deep inside her. Logan gently removed her fingers and held Faith's trembling body until she relaxed.

"That was intense," she whispered to Faith.

"I'm not sure which one of us needed it more," Faith replied.

"I think it was even. We both needed a release."

"We haven't had much time together lately, but hopefully, that will change now that you have weekends off."

"That was definitely worth the wait."

"Yes, it was."

Logan turned to face Faith. "You know, I've been thinking. I think you and I should go away for a weekend."

"Where do you want to go?" Faith asked.

"I'd like to see the ocean. I've been as far as the city, but that's it. We could leave Friday after work and be at the coast in three hours."

Faith reached out to Logan. Her fingers trailed along her lips. "I'd like that. Do you want to plan something while the kids are on break?"

"I know it will be too cold to get in the water, but I'd still like to walk on the beach with you."

"Do you think your dad would babysit Finder?"

"Yes, but it may be hard to get her back. You know Dad will spoil her rotten, right?"

"Everyone deserves a bit of spoiling."

"That's true. Maybe we can do some planning this weekend."

"I'd like that. We better get some sleep now, so we'll be fresh tomorrow."

"Goodnight, my love."

"Goodnight. Thank you for tonight."

"My pleasure." Faith chuckled.

"Mine, too."

CHAPTER FOURTEEN

Tommy delivered Chuck's truck, and they placed it into a spot near the shop. When Tommy left, Curtis looked at Logan. "Should we pop the hood and give her a once over?"

"I was hoping you'd say that. I'll finish the work on the lawn mower later." Logan opened the driver's door and pulled the hood latch.

Curtis lifted the hood. "Well, she's a bit too clean. No battery, no starter, or alternator. The engine doesn't have a lot of buildup on it. That's a powerful engine, too, if we can get it running again."

"If it ran out of oil, that might present a challenge, but we'll have to open her up to see for sure. We may need to rebuild it, but we have plenty of time. Chuck won't be able to get a full license for two years."

"If he rebuilds it with our supervision, there won't be much he won't be able to fix." Curtis removed his cap and ran a hand through his hair. "It will give us something to work on during the weekend. We usually aren't busy."

"I'll teach him how to use the credit card machine and cash register this week, and he can start on Saturday if that's okay."

Curtis nodded. "I think he should ride his bike in, and I will take him home when we close. He needs to build those muscles if he's going to be working here."

"If you could help us for a little while Saturday morning, we should be able to break the engine loose and lift it out. I've got a motor stand that hasn't gotten much use. We can place it on the stand while we work on it."

"That's no problem. Faith and I are making a supply run Saturday, so I can come help with that first. I'm making a delivery Saturday night."

"Will you return to get a nap before your run?"

"Yes, that shouldn't be a problem."

Logan smiled at her dad. "Faith and Patrice have a meal planned for the students, their families, and us. Could I talk you into making a large pan of your macaroni and cheese?"

"That should be easy enough. I'll make a list of supplies I'll need if y'all pick them up for me Saturday."

Logan nodded. "Faith and I are going to get a couple of the honey-baked hams, and Cal and Patrice are frying turkeys. The families and guests will be asked to bring sides."

"Is there anything else I can take?"

"I'll wait until Faith gets her menu arranged, and if we're short on anything, I'll let you know. On second thought, how about a pan of your corn casserole, too?"

"Those are both easy, so sign me up."

A car arrived at the gas pumps. "I'll get this," Logan said.

When she returned, she asked, "Are there any supplies we need here?"

"A case or two of oil and some spark plugs. Moon pies, too."

"Those were a given. I'm as hooked on them as you are." Logan chuckled.

†

Logan busied herself, stocking the oil and filters as Curtis took inventory of what they needed. They were running low on belts and antifreeze, too.

The school van pulled up, and Chuck came barreling into the garage.

"Whoa, slow your roll, little man," Logan teased. "Go put your backpack in the office. Faith will pitch a fit if we get oil on it."

"Yes, ma'am."

Curtis smiled at his excitement. "I know we're just basically looking today, but would you mind if I suggest you pull out a few of your old coveralls for Chuck to use, so he doesn't ruin his clothes?"

"It will free up some closet space for me. I'll pick some out tonight. Faith and I are going to his home tomorrow for dinner. I'll give them to him then, and he can wear a set Saturday. Teresa may need to make a few alterations."

Chuck raced back out to the garage. "What are we doing today?"

"We're going to do an assessment on your truck needs." Logan looked at him and pointed to a notepad. "Grab that, and let's get started."

For the next hour, they inspected the truck, and Chuck made a list of all the parts he would need to get her running again.

"The most important thing we need to determine first is if we can rebuild the engine. We won't know that until we take it out and open it up. Logan is going to help us remove it Saturday morning."

"On your off day?" Chuck asked.

"This part will take all three of us working together, but hopefully, it won't take long. Dad and I will clean and lubricate the motor mounts tomorrow and let them sit overnight. If we're lucky, they won't be a bear to remove on Saturday."

"What happens if we can't break one loose?"

"Worst case scenario, we use a torch to cut the mount. I hope it doesn't come to that. That would be a royal pain in the ass."

Curtis placed a hand on his shoulder. "We'll break them loose. Have faith."

"Speaking of Faith," Logan said, "go look at what she printed for you. It's on the desk. Grab your bag, and I'll take you home."

Chuck dashed toward the office. "We can do this, right?"

"A little late to be asking, but yes, I don't see anything we can't handle."

"I know it won't be a quick project. Patience may be the most difficult thing for Chuck to learn."

"That's important to learn, too." Curtis smiled.

"How about some grilled ham and cheese sandwiches tonight?"

"That's perfect, Dad. After that lunch, I don't think we need anything heavy."

†

Chuck walked out and hugged Logan. "Thank you for the picture. I'll hang it up in my room."

"Goodnight, Chuck. I'll see you at seven on Saturday," Curtis said and walked toward the office.

"I'll be here," Chuck called after him.

"Let's roll," Logan said.

She drove Chuck home and dropped him at his front door. "Please tell your mom we'll be out tomorrow night as soon as possible for supper. I'll need to go home and shower."

"I'll let her know. She's really excited that y'all are coming out. I can't wait to tell her about the Thanksgiving Feast the school will be hosting. I don't remember ever having real turkey, especially not a fried one. We only got TV dinners for Thanksgiving and Christmas," he said.

"You are in for a true surprise then. There will be all kinds of food for you to try."

Chuck opened the door and stepped out of the truck. "Thank you, Logan."

"You're welcome. See you tomorrow night."

†

The Thanksgiving Feast planners met for two hours after school. "I think we have a good plan in place," Patrice said. "Miss Betsy made a good point about the hams. It will be much less expensive to cook our own."

"I'm glad she offered to bake them. Logan and I are going on a supply run this weekend. If we find two nice ones, we'll pick them up and take them to Miss Betsy."

209

Patrice laughed as she opened her car door. "Cal has already bought two huge turkeys and the oil for frying. I think he's a bit excited."

"I don't think he's the only one. I wouldn't be surprised if many kids have never had the kind of food they will have on Thanksgiving. I heard Chuck telling Mike they only had turkey TV dinners."

"That's sad," Patrice said.

"Should we pick up some disposable plates and platters?"

"That probably wouldn't hurt. Do you need some money?"

"No, since we're doing our hams, it will be much cheaper, so Logan and I will get those supplies."

"I hope the kids will give the invitations to their parents tonight so we can get a headcount and an idea of what people will be bringing."

Faith chuckled. "As excited as they are, I bet that's the first thing they do when they get home."

"I know it's too late for Thanksgiving, but maybe we can have the kids do some Christmas skits or sing carols."

"They would enjoy that. My littles would make some adorable elves. We could get some help with sewing costumes if we buy the materials. Lord knows I can't sew a stitch, but I know some women who can."

Patrice hugged Faith. "I don't know about you, but I don't think teaching has ever been this much fun."

"I'd have to agree with you. It's nice to have the freedom to control what happens here, and the kids and families are so appreciative."

"I'll see you in the morning."

Finder rushed over to Faith with her ball. They watched Patrice drive away and walked to the shed. She swung the door open, and it didn't take long to find the dolly she and Logan could use to move the Holy Water. Faith tossed the ball and rolled the dolly to the porch.

†

After supper, Curtis left the kitchen and came back carrying a book. "Look what I found. It's not the exact manual for his motor, but it's close enough for him to study. It will help him understand what we need to do. Will you take it to him tomorrow night?"

Logan shook her head. "No, I think you should give it to him Saturday. If he gets it tomorrow, he may not sleep."

"Good point." Curtis chuckled. "I was thinking today how excited you were when we worked on Lightning. I see that same look in Chuck's eyes when we talk about the truck."

"I know, I see it, too. Chuck's such a good kid."

"It's fun to have another project to work on with a young'n," Curtis said.

"Yes, it is, Dad." She cleaned the kitchen. "I think I'm going to shower and call it a night."

"Goodnight, sweetheart."

"Goodnight, Dad."

†

Faith was excited when the kids arrived, and all the families but one would be participating. Mike was almost disappointed that his family would go to his grandma's for

211

Thanksgiving. "I can still help with the decorations, right?" he asked.

"Yes, you can, Mike. I would appreciate it if you would decorate the table for me, Logan's dad, and Logan."

"Someone needs to make one for Cal and me. Toby, his mom, and Miss Betsy, too," Patrice said.

"Logan and I will get the paper this weekend, so you will all have plenty of time to finish."

"What's our headcount?" Patrice asked.

"Thirty-two, if everyone shows. Curtis will make his macaroni and cheese and corn casserole, so we can add those to our food lists."

"I know we will have enough meat, but are we missing anything?"

"Desserts and casseroles are well covered. Miss Betsy is going to make four dozen deviled eggs. I think Miss Ruth is doing the rolls and several pies."

"Let me know if it looks like we need to add anything."

"We can always use more vegetables if you want to give them some thought. I may add a few things as well."

"I know we have ten days, but they will go quickly," Patrice said.

"Yes, they will. I'm glad we've got some excellent helpers."

"Me, too," Patrice agreed.

†

Logan finished up the lawn mower repair and sharpened the blades while Curtis cleaned and lubricated the motor mounts on Chuck's truck. Several customers stopped for gas and were excited about the Thanksgiving Day meal.

"It's going to be great fun," Logan promised.

When Curtis made a lunch run, Logan gassed Lightning and topped off her fluids. She would need to do an oil change in the next few weeks. Maybe Logan could get Chuck to help her one day after school. She looked over at the pile of coveralls she had put in her truck. Some were almost ten years old, but they should be small enough to fit Chuck. Teresa might need to tack up the legs, but he would grow into them once he started working with her dad. Curtis would work him hard, but he'd also make sure he was well fed.

Curtis returned carrying a bag. "Miss Ruth wouldn't make a club for you today. She insisted you have her chicken and dumplings, corn, and green beans. She even made corn muffins."

"The ones that look like mini ears of corn?" Logan asked.

"Exactly." Curtis grinned.

"You're going to Teresa's tonight, right?"

"Yes, sir. Do you need something?"

"Nope. I'll have a light dinner and then make my shopping lists for you this weekend. Add a couple dozen eggs. I'd like to make some pickled eggs."

"I'd buy them from Ray if you don't mind. He said his wife's hens are laying like crazy. Will you give him a call and get three dozen for me?"

"That shouldn't be a problem."

†

Teresa fed them a great meal, and Logan thought she would explode. When they finished, Teresa turned to the kids.

213

"Would y'all mind watching television for a while, and then we'll have some dessert?"

"Sure, Ma. Come on, Sades." He reached for his sister's hand.

Teresa looked at Logan and Faith. "There is something I'd like to ask the two of you."

"Sure, go ahead," Faith said.

"Given the recent events, I need to make some plans. We got some insurance money for Jerry, but it won't last forever. I created trust accounts for the kids to allow them to go to college or give them a good start on life after graduation."

"That was a smart decision," Logan said.

"I don't have any family other than my elderly mother. I'd like the two of you to become guardians to the kids in case something happens to me before they turn eighteen. I don't expect anything, but I need to create a will, and I'd like to add that clause."

Faith looked at Logan, who was smiling brightly. "We'd be delighted."

Logan nodded her head. "Just don't plan on going anywhere for a long time, but I agree it's good to be prepared."

Teresa sighed. "Thank you. I can't think of anyone better to entrust the kids with. I'll ask the lawyer if there is any paperwork we need to complete. That's a huge relief for me."

"We are delighted to be able to help. We think the world of both kids."

"Chuck said he's already learned more from the two of y'all than he has his entire life so far. He really looks up to you, Logan. And Sadie comes home raving about what she did in school. I've never seen her so excited."

"Would you mind if I call them back in now? I've got something for Chuck. Was there anything else we needed to discuss?" Logan asked.

"No. Thank you both, once again. Hey kids, come back to the kitchen, please."

Chuck and Sadie raced back in. "Is it time for dessert?"

"Yes, but I think Logan has something for you," Teresa told him.

"Run out to Lightning and bring in the stack of clothes in the back seat, please."

Chuck cocked his head, then walked out of the house.

"Clothes?" Teresa asked.

"Some of my old coveralls that might fit him, so he doesn't ruin his good clothes working with us. You may need to do a few alterations, especially in the inseam, but I'd tack the hems up because you know he'll grow into them."

Chuck rushed back into the house. "Are you kidding me? These are for me?"

"They aren't new, but they are well broken in. We don't want you to ruin your good clothes working at the shop."

"Can I try them on?" he asked his mom.

"Sure. Logan said you may need a few alterations so they fit well."

"I'll be right back." Chucked jogged down the hall to his bedroom.

"They still have my name patch on them, but I'll look into getting a few for him," Logan said.

"I seriously doubt he will worry about that. If you couldn't tell, he's a bit excited."

"We can get a bit dirty sometimes," Logan said.

Teresa smiled when Chuck returned. "I'll turn those sleeves up a bit and the legs, too, but I'm sure you'll be wearing them with no problems."

"Thanks, Ma. Thank you, Logan."

"I've got some spare room in my closet now, so I can pick up some new jeans. I'll need them if I'm going to have a social life," Logan said with a wink to Faith.

Teresa rolled the pant legs up to the point she needed to tack them up. "Go take them off carefully, and I'll hem them tonight. You start work tomorrow morning, right?"

"Yes, ma'am." Chuck's face was beaming when he left the kitchen.

"Who wants pie?" Teresa asked.

"Bring it on," Logan replied.

†

"That was an unexpected surprise," Faith said when they climbed into bed.

"Yes, it was. I had no clue. I think we'd make good parents if we had to step into the role."

"I do, too. I hope we can continue to help and we don't have to do that. I'm proud of how well Teresa is adapting and making great decisions for the future."

"Me, too. Many people would blow through that money with no regard for the future. It's refreshing that she's putting the kids' needs before hers."

Faith snuggled into Logan. "What time do you plan to go to the shop?"

"I thought I'd go early, so I can come back to shower before we go to town. I'd like to make it back from the deliveries in time for a nap since I'm making a run tomorrow night."

"Why don't we drop the supplies off at the shop and come back here? I can separate the food for the families and then deliver it while you nap."

"If we run late, I may take you up on that, but I prefer to help you."

"I know you do, but I want you alert tonight. I've already moved everything to the base of the steps. You were right. It's so much easier with the dolly."

"Doubling the order is a good thing, but it's twice the weight, and it takes up every inch of space in the compartment."

"Is it too much?"

"No, I'd rather deliver a bigger order than have to risk twice as many runs."

"I agree. I'm on pins and needles until I know you are safely home."

"I promise I won't take unnecessary risks."

"Thank you," Faith murmured against her skin.

Logan could feel Faith's body relax and softly kissed the top of her head.

CHAPTER FIFTEEN

Faith sorted the bags of supplies they had purchased while Logan took a shower. When Logan walked into the kitchen, Faith had finished her chore. "Are you sure you don't need my help?"

"I'm positive. You have done a lot today and need to be rested for tonight." Faith walked over and kissed Logan. "I'll wake you at nine, and we can have a late dinner before we load the truck and get you on the road."

"That sounds great. Removing that motor took more effort than I thought it would. I don't need anything heavy, though, after that lunch. Honestly, I'd be okay with warming up the leftovers."

"That wouldn't be a problem. Maybe I'll make a dessert then."

"Now, you are singing my tune." Logan chuckled. "I love you."

"Love you, too. Have a good nap."

218

†

Faith loaded the bags and boxes into the back seat of her car. She stopped by the station to top off her gas, and Chuck raced out to meet her.

"Hey, Ms. Faith. You need gas?"

"Yes, sir, I do. Fill it up, please."

"Do you need me to check your oil?"

Faith knew there was no need to check it since Logan had recently done an oil change, but he was excited. "That would be great." She popped the hood and walked inside to find Curtis.

"Hey, Faith," Curtis called from the garage bay.

"Hey, Curtis. How's Chuck doing?"

Curtis wiped his face. "He's a quick learner and has such energy. He makes me tired just watching him. He was here at a quarter to seven this morning."

"I've got deliveries to make. Do you want me to drop Chuck at home for you?"

"That would be great. Let Chuck help you with the deliveries, though."

Chuck rushed over to them. "Your oil is good. Your car took twenty dollars."

Faith reached into her pocket for a twenty and handed it to him.

"Faith needs your help with some deliveries, so she'll drop you at home if that's okay with you?"

Chuck scratched his head. "What about my bike?"

"You can put it in the back of my truck. I'll drop it off at your house and let your ma know you'll be home a little later."

"Sounds great. I'll ring up the sale, load my bike, and be ready," he told Faith.

219

Faith smiled at Curtis. "I see what you mean about his energy level. Did you get much done on the motor today?"

"We started breaking it down. It's got some wear and will need a lot of work, but nothing we can't do with time and some money. Once it's rebuilt, it will last him a long time if he takes good care of it."

Faith observed Chuck place his bike in the bed of Curtis' truck. "I feel confident he will take care of it. He's so excited."

Curtis nodded. "I found a manual that is relatively close to his engine size. I bet he'll be up late reading it tonight."

"That's one way of getting him to practice reading and learn new words." Faith nodded.

"I feel he will come in with a hundred questions tomorrow."

"Thank you for being so patient with him."

"He's a great kid and a hard worker. I could easily see him replacing me when I retire."

"Many years down the road," Faith said.

"I hope."

Chuck was waiting beside her car. "I guess that's my cue to get moving. I'll see you later."

"Be safe and have fun," Curtis called after her.

"Ready to ride?" she asked Chuck.

"Yes, ma'am. What are we delivering?"

"You see those bags in the back seat?"

"I do. Are these like the bags you bring to our house every month?"

"Yes. Logan and I buy supplies for the families in our community and deliver them. It's something my grandfather started years ago."

"I've never seen Ma give you any money."

"You won't see me accept any either, Chuck. We do this for the community out of goodwill."

He stared into the backseat for several long minutes. "That must cost a lot of money."

"It's worth every cent we spend."

"I know we appreciate your help. You always put something special in for us."

"We try," Faith said with a wink. Faith turned on her turn signal. "Will you take the bags to the door for me?"

"Yes, ma'am."

Faith parked in front of the first house and told Chuck which bags to take. She watched as he carried them up to the door and knocked. When the door opened, he was welcomed into the house, and Miss Betsy waved at Faith.

Chuck raced back out to the car and climbed in. "I put them on the table for Miss Betsy. I hope that was okay."

"Perfect. Most of the families will be at home. If you knock and don't get an answer, we leave them on the doorstep."

Faith and Chuck made deliveries to six homes. "What's next?"

"Your home," Faith said. "Thanks for your help. You made the deliveries go fast for me today."

"I'll help you anytime you need, Ms. Faith."

"Thank you. I might take you up on that."

Chuck smiled at her as she turned into his driveway. His bike was parked next to the front porch. "The rest of the bags are for your ma. Do you need help?"

"No, ma'am. I can get them. Thank you," he said when he saw a family-sized box of Cap'n Crunch. "Did you know that was my favorite?"

"I did. Actually, Logan did. She knew you liked them, and Sadie likes the strawberry pop tarts."

"We didn't use to get them before when Ma would shop." He smiled at Faith. "I've got a long way to go to pay Logan back for the truck, but when I start making some money, will you bring a few special things for us?"

"I'd be delighted. Just let me know what you need when you're ready."

"Thanks." Chuck picked up the bags and carried them onto the porch. Teresa stepped out to help him and waved at Faith.

†

Logan slowed down, preparing to turn off the highway, when she saw a flash of color in her headlights. Intuition told her to keep going, and when she passed the vehicle, she recognized it as a county deputy. Logan kept driving and reached down to turn on the police scanner to see if she could pick up on the chatter. Logan pulled onto a side trail a quarter of a mile down the road and parked in a grove of thick trees. The scanner crackled with the communications of a couple of state troopers on the interstate who were meeting up for a meal break. It must be an uneventful night if they were meeting for a break. She waited for several more minutes, but the radio remained silent. Logan would have to make a decision. She could continue to the drop site and make the delivery, then circle back to pick up the payment, or she could wait and see if there was any movement by the deputy. Given his position, Logan was confident that it was a coincidence that he had parked in the turnoff where the payment was located. She was sure he would be concealed farther down the path if he had spotted the drop box. Logan weighed her options and decided to make the delivery. Even if she was stopped with the money, she could claim it was revenue from the garage she would deposit, but a truckload

222

of Holy Water would bring deep trouble. Logan started her motor and pulled onto the road without headlights. She would drive several hundred yards before turning them on to delay detection if the deputy was looking to his right. She moved quickly, and when she hit her headlights, she sped away into the dark night.

Logan turned onto the dark path that led to the drop zone and kept her senses alert to any movement or sound. She could hear her heart racing as she unloaded the delivery and snapped the lock on the box. She tossed the camouflage netting over to conceal the location and raced back to the truck. Logan was relieved to make the drop. The hairs on her arms stood on end as she climbed back into the truck and heard the scanner crackle.

"I have a feeling we might see the Ghost tonight," a voice announced across the airwaves.

"Not if I see you first," Logan said.

Logan knew if she could carefully pick her way through the woods, she could get close enough to hike to the money box to retrieve the payment. Eventually, the deputy would go back on patrol, but Logan didn't want to have to wait him out. She cranked the truck and began easing her way through the trees. If she could retrieve the payment, Logan could use the back roads to make it home without being seen.

When she thought she was as close as she dared to drive, Logan parked and waited several minutes before leaving the truck's safety. She wove her way carefully through the trees, and it only took ten minutes to reach the drop box. Logan removed the envelope and replaced the camouflage to conceal the spot. Halfway back to the truck, she heard branches snapping and froze in her tracks. She was squatting to hide her location, her eyes scanning her surroundings and her ears on alert to any sound. Logan heard the sound again, behind her this time. She swiveled to see a doe and her fawn walking through the woods. Logan remained still for several minutes to allow the pair time to move away before she continued back to her truck. When Lightning came into view, Logan let out a sigh of relief. As she reached for the door handle, she heard the sound of a siren echoing through the woods. It was difficult to tell which direction it was traveling, so Logan climbed into the truck and lowered a window. The siren was fading, so Logan knew it was moving away from her.

"I think it's the Ghost," an excited voice came over the scanner.

"Stick with him and let's bring him in tonight," another voice answered.

"Roger that."

Logan cranked her truck and eased through the woods until she reached a county road. It was time to begin scouting out a new delivery route. Tonight was a bit too close for comfort. Logan hit her headlights and hauled ass back to Faith's.

†

Faith woke when Logan climbed into the bed. "Sorry I'm so late."

"Did you run into problems?"

Logan nodded. "A county guy was sitting at the entrance of the money box. I had to make the drop first and then crawl through the woods to sneak back in to grab the money. It's time to scout out a new drop area."

"We haven't changed in a while, so we're probably past due."

"Yeah. Tonight was too close for comfort," Logan admitted.

"There's no need to be up early in the morning, is there?"

"Not for me. Finder will probably be the first one awake," Logan teased.

"I'll sneak out with her and try to stay quiet while you sleep."

"Crawl back into bed with me if you can," Logan said. She wrapped her body around Faith's. "You're toasty warm," she whispered.

"Welcome home, baby," Faith answered and scooted even closer.

CHAPTER SIXTEEN

The students worked hard on the decorations for the Thanksgiving Feast. The cafeteria was beautiful when they were done, and the table coverings turned out fantastic. When school ended for the holiday break on Friday, the students were excited about returning Thursday. Last-minute arrangements were made, and the school was buzzing with activity on Thursday. Cal and Curtis had the turkey fryers set up and ready to cook. Toby helped his mother and Miss Betsy deliver the hams and other goods. They had agreed to eat family style, so Elizabeth and some of the older students set the tables. They had two long tables for the meal and a separate table for desserts. Families began arriving and the air filled with delicious aromas.

Curtis carried in the first of the fried turkeys. "After this one cools for a few minutes, I'll come and begin carving them," he told Faith.

"You and Toby can start on the hams after that while Cal finishes the final turkey," Faith answered.

"I'll be Cal's gopher," Logan volunteered.

Patrice and Faith looked at the rapidly filling tables. There would be plenty of food and probably some leftovers the families could take home.

Patrice smiled at Faith. "This is going to be so good."

Faith nodded. "I don't think anyone will go home hungry today."

"While you are waiting, you can get a head start on the rest of us by writing what you are thankful for this year," Patrice told the families that had already found their seats. "We want to keep these table sheets for the kids to see throughout the rest of the school year," she explained.

Teresa handed Chuck and Sadie a crayon and began writing her note of thanks. Other families took their lead and followed.

Curtis and Logan placed platters piled high with ham and turkey on each table. "There's even more we can add once this disappears," Curtis told Patrice. "I'll go ahead and finish the hams. The last turkey will need to cool once Cal brings it inside."

"Save the hambones," Faith reminded him. "I'm sure we'll have someone who wants them to season a pot of beans."

Curtis chuckled. "Miss Ruth has already claimed dibs on one of them. She wants to make a huge pot of beans for everyone next week."

"With some of her cracklin' cornbread, onion slices, and sweet pickles, I hope," Faith said.

"Don't you know it," Curtis answered.

"That sounds like something that would be worth driving out for. When is Miss Ruth cooking?" Patrice asked.

227

"Sunday for supper. Faith and Logan are taking a short trip, so she will cook when they return," Curtis shared. "My mouth is watering already."

When Cal and Logan brought the second turkey in to cool, Faith asked everyone to take their seats. "I would like to ask Miss Betsy to bless this meal for us. I would also like to remind you to share something you are thankful for this year on the table covers before you leave today. Before I forget, thank you all for coming and bringing a dish to share."

Miss Betsy stood to bless the food. "I would like to thank you and Patrice for organizing this feast for the families and everyone who helped make it wonderful. Now, if you would, please bow your heads."

Platters were passed, and plates were filled with food. It was challenging to determine which foods were enjoyed the most. The fried turkeys were a new experience for most families, and Faith thought they turned out fantastic.

"I can't wait to try a sandwich made with this turkey," she told Cal. "It's delicious."

Cal nodded. "It's all fantastic. I've never seen so many of my favorites at one time."

When Logan declared she was full, Chuck handed her a crayon. "Thanks for the reminder."

The tables were cleared as people began to enjoy the desserts. Faith, Miss Betsy, and Patrice began making carry-home containers of food.

"I can't believe there is this much left," Logan said as she brought a platter of deviled eggs into the kitchen. "Minus one more," she said, placing the egg in her mouth.

Faith handed her a few empty containers. "Make us some leftovers, please."

†

Miss Ruth handed them a cup of coffee. "Get your desserts and come relax. We can finish up later."

"How am I supposed to decide?" Logan declared when she picked up a plate at the dessert table.

"Take a little bit of everything that looks good to you," Faith suggested.

"Do we have any turkey platters left? It all looks so good."

Patrice whispered to Faith, "Should we ask everyone to share what they were thankful for?"

"I think we can ask if they would like to share," Faith said. Faith picked out several desserts and walked back to her seat.

Patrice sat across from her. "If everyone has their desserts, I would like you to share what you have written on your table if you are willing to share."

Elizabeth immediately raised her hand. "I'd like to be the first to thank you and Miss Faith for starting this school. This has been the most fun and educational experience ever."

"We don't have to ride that stinking bus for hours either," Mike added.

Several people laughed softly at his comment.

"I'd like to thank this community for coming together to make this a great feast," Miss Ruth said.

"I love picking up the kids and taking them home at the end of their day. Their excitement is contagious," Toby added.

There was a multitude of thanks for the school and the meal. Others were grateful for good health and a bountiful harvest, but Chuck's comment made Faith's breath catch and many sets of eyes water. It was a simple yet powerful message.

Chuck turned to his mom. "I am thankful for my mom being brave."

The room was silent as Teresa hugged Chuck. "I am thankful for two wonderful children."

"I'm thankful for strawberry pop tarts," Sadie added, making everyone laugh.

Everyone turned to Logan. She cleared her throat. "I am thankful to be a part of such a caring community."

Faith turned to Patrice. "I'm thankful for you coming into our lives and making this project a reality for our students and our family."

Patrice smiled. "I'm thankful to be accepted into this loving community and allowed to learn from you."

Cal was grateful for meeting Patrice and being allowed to participate in the school activities.

Curtis was last. "I'll be even more grateful for seconds on desserts," he claimed.

Everyone laughed and cheered when he led the rush back to the dessert table.

Logan looked over at the note he had scribbled. *I am grateful for the best two daughters a man could ask for.* She swallowed hard and picked up her plate. "I shouldn't, but that banana pudding is calling my name."

"I'm right behind you," Cal said.

Faith looked at Patrice. "We did well."

Patrice nodded. "Yes, we did."

†

After the final clean up and everyone had left with at least another meal for everyone in their family, Logan picked up their containers. "It's time for us to go crash," she told Faith. "Finder is probably waiting to go potty."

Faith shook her head. "Nope, she's been out playing fetch with Chuck for the last half hour. She's probably asleep on the porch by now."

"Let's go home and see." Logan reached for Faith's hand.

Finder was sleeping in front of the door, and she lifted her head when she heard them approach. "Dad is so excited to babysit for us," Logan said. "I hope he doesn't spoil her too bad the next two days."

Faith smirked. "Like she could be much more spoiled."

"I don't know. Dad will probably have her sleeping in bed with him."

"Nope, we are taking her bed with specific instructions," Faith said. "I don't want her to become a bed hog, and she's comfy in her own bed."

"I will leave that conversation to you and Dad."

Finder stood and stretched. "Go potty, sleepyhead, and let's go inside." Faith leaned down to stroke her head as she climbed down the steps.

Logan walked inside and saw the suitcases and the pile of dog supplies stacked by the front door. "You realize we will only be gone until midday Sunday, right?"

"Yes, but I didn't know what to pack for us. I'm sure it will be cooler on the coast than here."

"That's true. It is getting cooler. Would you mind if I go ahead and load the truck?"

"Not at all. I'm as excited as you are. I hope we can get an early start in the morning. We can't check into the hotel until three, but I'm sure we can find plenty to see until then."

"No doubt," Logan said and picked up the suitcases.

Faith placed the food in the refrigerator and prepared Finder's dinner. "Are you hungry, baby girl?"

Logan picked up the box with Finder's supplies. "We can't forget to pack Bear-Bear for her tomorrow when we take her bed out."

"I know. Finder sleeps with him every night."

When Logan returned, Faith smiled at her. "I need a shower. Care to join me?"

"I'd be delighted."

†

Logan woke to find Faith busy in the kitchen. "What are you doing?"

"I thought we'd have turkey sandwiches today to use the rest of the leftovers."

"That sounds great to me." She leaned down to kiss Faith. "Do you need me to get your picnic basket?"

"Please," Faith replied. "I'll start making breakfast if you want to shower and dress."

"Deal. I'll bring Bear-Bear and Finder's bed, so we don't forget."

Faith loaded the picnic basket while Logan placed the dog bed and stuffed toy by the front door. Finder looked at her and walked over to pick up her toy. "We won't forget him. I promise," Logan said. "You're going to spend the weekend with your grandpa."

Finder curled up in her bed with Bear-Bear blocking the door. She was sure they weren't going anywhere without her.

"Will she be okay with your dad?"

232

"I'm sure she will. Chuck will be there, too, so she'll have someone to play with during the day." Logan noticed the look of concern on Faith's face. "She will be just fine, Mama. I'll be right back."

†

Faith had tears in her eyes when they dropped Finder off to Curtis. Logan transferred her food and supplies into his truck.

"I promise, Chuck and I will take good care of her." Curtis smiled at Faith.

"I know you will, but this will be the first time we've been apart since she found me," Faith stammered.

"Give her a hug, get in the truck, and have some fun. We will be fine here," Curtis told her.

"I will be back to get you, baby girl," Faith said, kissing the top of Finder's head and hugging her. "I'll call to check on her."

"That's fine. I'll send you some pictures if Chuck can teach me how to take pictures on this phone."

"That's no problem, Mr. Bronson," Chuck answered. "I'll make sure you get pics."

"Thanks, Chuck," Logan answered. "Y'all have fun."

"You, too," Curtis said. "Bring us something from the beach."

"We will." Logan hugged her dad and walked to the truck with Faith.

Faith looked out the side view mirror. Finder stood between Curtis and Chuck. She was wagging her tail and then chased after Chuck when he grabbed her ball.

Logan watched Faith's response. "See, she's going to be just fine." She reached over for Faith's hand.

233

Faith scooted over toward Logan. "I know she's in good hands."

"So are you." Logan smiled and wrapped her arm around Faith.

Logan had studied the road map carefully. She had never driven to the coast and marveled at the change of scenery they passed as she went. The mountains turned into foothills and then flatland. Logan could feel the difference in temperatures as they drove. "Are you getting cool? I can roll up the windows."

"No, I'm fine. I love the different scents. I bet we start smelling salt soon," Faith said.

"I've never seen the ocean, so I have no idea what to expect."

"Water as far as your eyes can see. There may be boats on the water as fishermen come in with their morning catches or go out for the day. I don't imagine there will be people in the water this time of year, but they may be walking the beach looking for shells."

†

Logan was silent for several minutes contemplating Faith's words. "There it is. We must be getting close."

"Yes, we can't be far now. Let's drive down the beach and find a covered table. I'm kinda hungry."

They drove past several hotels, and Faith pointed out the one they would stay in.

"That looks nice, and there are several restaurants close. I'd love to treat you to some fresh seafood. It's right across from the beach, too."

"It doesn't get any fresher than this," Faith agreed.

Logan continued driving, passing a small marina filled mostly with pleasure boats. A mile farther down the road, she found a picnic area covered by a pavilion. "Is this good?"

"That looks like a perfect spot."

Logan carried the picnic basket to the table and returned for the cooler. It was difficult for her to tear her eyes away from the dark blue ocean in front of them. "Kick off your shoes, roll up your pant legs, and walk down to the beach. I'll get lunch ready for us," Faith offered.

Logan didn't need further prompting. She took her shoes off and quickly rolled her jeans up to her knees.

"Go," Faith said and shooed her away from the table. She watched Logan walk quickly between the dunes down to the beach. Logan pulled up short before reaching the water and bent over to inspect something lying on the beach. Cautiously she approached an incoming wave and allowed the water to rush across her feet. Faith smiled when she heard the sound of shock in Logan's voice and began preparing lunch.

†

Even with Faith's warning, Logan hadn't expected such a vast expanse of water. It was cold as it rushed over her feet, and she wondered if it would be refreshing in the heat of the summer. She bent down, let the water rush through her fingers, and brought one to her lips. Definitely salty. Large brown pelicans bobbed in the water beyond the breakers, searching for their own meal. Gulls screeched as they flew behind a small boat, diving and squabbling for scraps of food tossed overboard. *Noisy buggers,* she thought as she looked up at the sky. It was a deep blue, almost as blue as the water, with streaks of white, evidence of a jet flying through to its destination. Logan was mesmerized by the sounds until laughter filled the air, and she looked farther down the beach. Four young people clad in wetsuits jogged toward the water carrying surfboards. *That's dedication or insanity,* she thought as she watched them mount their boards and paddle away from the shore. The waves looked small to Logan, but they generated enough power to speed the surfers toward the shore. She enjoyed how they shifted their weight to guide the boards through the water. She laughed with them when one took a spill into the cold water.

"They must be crazy," Faith spoke as she approached. "That water has to be frigid."

"I sure wouldn't want to spend time in it," Logan said as she turned toward her. "It is beautiful, though. Different than I had imagined, but in a good way."

"Are you ready to eat? We can walk down the beach afterward."

"I am hungry." Logan smiled. She reached for Faith's hand, and they walked back to the pavilion. Logan bit into a sandwich and smiled at Faith after she swallowed. "You remembered the cranberry sauce. Thank you."

"You've got me convinced a turkey sandwich is naked without cranberry sauce and dressing." Faith poured some chips on her plate and handed the bag to Logan.

†

"I definitely need a long walk after eating all that. Thank you for a great meal," Logan said. "I swear that turkey tastes better every time I eat it."

"Cal can fry a turkey for us anytime. That was delicious." Faith packed up the picnic basket and carried it to the truck. "Are you ready for a walk?"

"Almost." Logan rushed to the back of the truck and returned with a bucket. She smiled at Faith and shrugged. "In case we find something."

"We will probably need to get out here early to beat the beachcombers to the good shells," Faith stated. "You never know, though."

She reached for Faith's hand. "Which way do you want to go?"

"Let's go right. Maybe there haven't been folks out here before us. I think the surfers have decided to call it a day."

They walked down the beach hand in hand, stopping to examine shells and pieces of driftwood. They found several small seashells intact that Logan gently placed in the bucket. They had walked for almost an hour when Faith frowned and pointed across the water. "I think we'd better head back to the truck. It looks like a storm is blowing in."

"Are you afraid we'll melt?" Logan teased.

"No, but I'm sure it will be a cold rain."

"Good point," Logan said, and they rushed back to the truck.

†

"It's still a bit early for check-in. Do you want to ride in the other direction and see if we can find some souvenirs for Dad and Chuck?"

"That sounds great. Chuck sent me several pictures already. Finder looks just fine."

"See, I told you she would be fine."

Logan pulled into a shop, and they walked inside as the rain began to fall. "That was great timing," Faith said.

237

"It's just an afternoon squall. It will move through fast," a woman behind the counter said. "Welcome, and take your time browsing."

"Thanks," Logan said. She and Faith walked the aisles of the store. "What do you think about this for Chuck?" Logan held a leather necklace with a shark's tooth dangling from the bottom.

"Do you think that's a genuine shark tooth?" Faith asked.

"The tag claims it is." Logan smiled. "I wouldn't want to get close enough to see who was missing teeth."

"Sharks actually shed their teeth often to make way for new ones," the woman stated. "I think that may be a tiger shark tooth you're holding," she said, looking over the bridge of her glasses. "The smaller ones may be Mako or reef sharks."

"I think he would like anything his hero gave him," Faith teased. "What would your dad like?"

"He could use a new ball cap. His are getting pretty worn."

"This one?" Faith held up a bright pink one.

"Lord, no. Not his color at all. That NASCAR one in blue would suit him just fine."

"I think these are good for starters. We may find something else later." Faith paid for their purchases, and they drove to the hotel to check in. The front desk clerk recommended two restaurants for seafood.

"Local spots, not chains." She winked at Faith. "Great spot for oysters, too, if you like them. They serve them raw and grilled in several different ways. Parmesan is my favorite. The shrimp are excellent, too."

"I'd like some fried shrimp," Faith replied.

"The portions are huge at a reasonable price."

"That sounds hard to beat."

"You won't go wrong at either place."

"Maybe we should try one tonight and the other tomorrow night?" Logan suggested.

"I'm game," Faith answered. "Let's get settled in and ready for dinner."

"Go early tonight. Folks will be tired of turkey and dressing and want something different," the clerk warned.

"Thanks," Logan said. "Let's roll."

†

"That was a delicious meal," Logan said as they drove back to the hotel.

"Yes, it was. I'm ready to relax and spend the night loving you. We have no need to rush and can enjoy our time together."

"That sounds like the perfect way to end a great day. I'm so glad we took this trip. We've never been anywhere together, which makes it more special."

"We need to agree to not get caught up, and do more together while we are young enough to enjoy it."

Logan chuckled. "I'd like to try surfing, but only when it's warmer."

"It did look like they were having fun. We'll need to start saving now. It will be much more expensive during the summer months."

"Money well spent," Logan said.

†

They made love deep into the night and fell asleep wrapped in one another's arms. Early the following day, Logan woke and glanced at the clock. It was still early enough for them to catch the sunrise on the beach. She leaned down to kiss Faith awake. "I need you to wake up and come with me," she whispered.

Faith groaned when she saw the time.

"Come on, let's go watch the sunrise. Then we can come back and sleep longer if you want. Bundle up it will be cold." When Faith had dressed, Logan helped her into a heavy coat. She grabbed a blanket from the closet and reached for Faith. "Ready?"

Faith nodded and smiled.

They stepped out into the chilly darkness, and Logan turned on a flashlight to guide their way through the dunes. She spotted a driftwood log a short way down the beach, and Faith took a seat and allowed Logan to wrap the blanket around them as she snuggled into her body. "It shouldn't be long now," Logan said as she could see the horizon begin to lighten. The blinking lights of the fishermen's boats flashed in the darkness as they headed out to sea. "Are you warm enough?"

"Yes, you're the best heater ever," Faith told Logan.

While they waited for the sun to arrive, Logan took Faith's hand underneath the blanket. "I have a confession to make."

Faith looked up at her. "What?"

"I fudged on my answer when I wrote that I was happy to be a part of the community. I mean, I am, but I am most thankful for the day that brought you home to me. I never realized I could be so happy with anyone. You've made all my dreams come true, and there is one more thing I want."

"What is that?"

"It's time for me to come home to you every night if you will still have me. Dad will be okay on his own. I know that now."

"Oh, Logan. I have waited forever to hear those words. I love you so much, and I want to begin every day of the rest of my life beside you." Faith leaned in and kissed Logan. The kiss turned into several, and Faith giggled when she realized they had nearly missed the sunrise. "It's so beautiful," Faith said as the first rays filled the low-hanging clouds.

"It doesn't hold a candle to how beautiful you are to me," Logan told Faith. "My world spins around you."

Faith saw the tears in Logan's eyes and felt hers watering. She snuggled into Logan's warmth, and they enjoyed the sunrise of the first day of the rest of their lives.

PERSONAL NOTES FROM THE AUTHOR

———————————————————————

Some of you know I frequently listen to music while I write, and the play list I created for this story seemed to grow every week. Even if you aren't a country music fan, or if you are, I'd like to introduce you to the songs that motivated me to write this story for you. Thank you to the artists who wrote and sang these songs.

Play List for Holy Water and Whiskey Scars

"Holy Water" by Michael Ray
"What my World Spins Around" by Jordan Davis
"Wait in the Truck" by Hardy and Lainey Wilson
"Son of a Sinner" by Jelly Roll
"So Many Skies" by Caroline Jones and Mathew Ramsey
"Rock and a Hard Place" by Bailey Zimmerman

"Growing Old With You" by Restless Road
"You Proof" by Morgan Wallen
"Midnight Rider's Prayer" by Brothers Osborne
"Skeletons" by Brothers Osborne
"Lone Wolf" by Eric Church
"Out in the Middle" by Zac Brown
"Water Under the Bridge" by Sam Hunt
"Middle of Somewhere" by Luke Combs
"Soul" by Lee Brice
"Don't Come Lookin'" by Jackson Dean
"Strangers" by Maddie and Tae
"The Kind of Love We Make" by Luke Combs

ABOUT THE AUTHOR
ALI SPOONER

Ali Spooner lives in beautiful northwest Florida with several fur babies. Ali's writing began as a hobby, and with the assistance of the Affinity Rainbow Publishing team has advanced her love of storytelling to a new level.

Ali's characters are primarily everyday people, from cowgirls to psychics. Ali also has created a few supernatural characters in her paranormal series. Several of her twenty-plus books have been Amazon-rated number one choices and always include a happily ever after. Ali's hobbies include photography, reading, travel, college sports, and spending time with family and friends.

OTHER AFFINITY BOOKS

Politics of Love by Annette Mori

Governor Sandra Murphy is rethinking the sanity of allowing her mother to talk her into considering becoming the democratic party's choice for the presidential nominee. Sandra has enough to contend with after surviving a bomb attack, thanks to the brave border control agent working alongside the clever undercover FBI agent. Now she has to worry about a pesky reporter who seems to be everywhere scoping stories Sandra would prefer Wynter Holmes steer far away from.

Wynter admires the charismatic governor. After all, she voted for the woman. But that doesn't give Governor Murphy a free pass. A breaking story is what Wynter lives for, and she isn't about to stop digging just because the engaging governor is attractive, single, and an out lesbian. Reporting for the famously biased, right-wing media conglomerate is not exactly making Wynter a friend of the enigmatic leader.

Will repeated attempts on Governor Murphy's life where Wynter might be collateral damage bring them closer together or tear them apart from what might be a perfect match?

Out and Loud by Ali Spooner

The Bentleys have begun celebrating their success by performing live in small venues and outdoor concerts. Their music and love for one another continue to grow as their number drops to four. Stone is needed at home to run the business during his father's rehabilitation, but the Bentleys drive forward. Cedra's challenge to her bandmates to create original songs for their next album turns into brilliant love songs, rockabilly, and a Pride Festival anthem. Ride along with the Bentleys as they capture the hearts of country music lovers across the nation.

Undercover Love by Annette Mori

When the domestic terrorist cell Emma Schmidt has infiltrated summons her to an abandoned warehouse for a loyalty test, Emma immediately recognizes the battered woman. Emma must act fast to protect her cover and save the woman, Jimena Aguilar, she's never forgotten.

Emma and Jimena team up on a dangerous mission to take down the terrorist cell and save the life of the popular California governor.

Will this lead them back to the closeness they once shared or have the years in between hardened their hearts to love.

Changing Times by Jen Silver

Thirty years on from when we first met Dani Barker and Camila Callaghan in *Changing Perspectives*, they're enjoying marriage and semi-retirement in a luxury flat near London.

Dani's niece, Holly, runs their mixed media business, now gaining a foothold in the highly competitive online games market. Holly's older sibling, Luc, influences people to take action on climate issues with their website, Gaia One: One Earth, One Chance.

Romance has been in short supply for both Holly and Luc. Immersed in her work, Holly's dating life is non-existent. For Luc, family prejudices stand in the way of a relationship with the love of their life.

Can Holly and Luc succeed in making the changes necessary to achieve their own happy ever afters?

Midnight in Nashville by Ali Spooner

The Bentleys have successfully finished cutting their first album, *Six Strings, and a Dream*. When the Covid-19 epidemic hits, tours and live performances are cancelled as the world goes into lockdown. With the closing of the restaurant, employment for the band members has been severely impacted. The group comes together to make life work at Ma Bentley's Boarding House. They take advantage of their down time and use of the studio to record more songs. Cedra has challenged each of her bandmates to create a song for their next album. Juliet's song, "Midnight in Nashville," is chosen as the title track. Join the group as they venture into new marketing avenues and create their first music video for the title track.

Compound Interest by Annette Mori

The kick-ass women in The Organization are back and they have their sights set on a few new recruits. Not everyone is jumping for joy at the choices, considering subterfuge is front and center in the games the new recruits have been playing.

Dani is supposed to get her happily ever after, but she's not sure what's real anymore including Candy's feelings for her. When a new enemy takes Candy captive, Dani vows to uncover the truth by insisting on going on the mission to save her. Candy is not what she seems, and that presents a new set of complications for Dani and her feelings.

The Organization continues to have challenges when those damn book magicians and book witches keep popping back in to warn them of new catastrophes on the horizon. She doesn't have time for their warnings, until their enemies intersect once again to keep them working together.

From award-winning author, Annette Mori, find out what happens in this final chapter of the combined Asset Management/Book Addict series.

Six Strings and a Dream by Ali Spooner

Cedra Tyler's dream of becoming a songwriter in Nashville was put on hold due to her mother's failing health. When the time came for Cedra to start her journey, she left her home in south Alabama with a heavy heart.

Arriving at Ma Bentley's boarding house, meeting her housemates, also fledgling musicians, she feels the warmth she was missing since leaving home.

Her housemates realize Cedra's talent as a song writer and begin to gel as a group. The pain and loss she had experienced added a layer of emotion and longing in her lyrics unusual for someone of her age.

They form a band, The Bentley's, named after Ma who is much more than a landlord to them all. Cedra falls for bandmate Juliet, and that inspires her creativity even more.

Will The Bentley's achieve their dream of making it big in Music City? Has Cedra found her forever in the arms of Juliet?

eBooks, Print, Free eBooks

Visit our website for more publications available online.

https://affinityebooks.com/

Published by Affinity Rainbow Publications
A Division of Affinity eBook Press NZ LTD
Canterbury, New Zealand

Registered Company 2517228

www.ingramcontent.com/pod-product-compliance
Lightning Source LLC
Chambersburg PA
CBHW060539260626
47161CB00003B/970